Where Once a Flower Grew

Willum Fowler

Mi Amor,
I just arrive. The trip was hard, and I no feel well.
I hurt for you so bad. I miss your face and your touch.
I miss your voice that comfort me so.
Please come for me as soon as possible.
Te Amo,
Flor

Chapter 1

Adam Clay looked out the window of American flight 609. Thirty thousand feet below, like a silver snake basking in the sun, lay the Rio Grande. Slowly, the river drifted aft, finally disappearing in a blue-white cloud bank. He looked up. The sky was crystal. He was now in Mexican air space…his destination, Mexico City.

He looked outward towards the distant horizon, his mind consumed by a single nagging thought…*Got to make it in time.*

He looked at his watch…a little after 8 a.m. Central.

"Damn you," he muttered, "Damn you all."

He glanced over at the man next to him. There, in his seat reclined back as far as it would go, he was sound asleep with his mouth open…*Lucky bastard…Probably all he has to worry about is getting home in time for dinner.*

All of a sudden he felt flush and started to sweat. It lasted less than a minute, but left him light-headed and drained.

"Sir, are you alright…can I get you anything?"

He looked up. The attractive young flight attendant had a concerned look on her face.

"No, thank you. I'm fine…well, maybe a little water," he said.

"I'll be right back." She smiled, which took a little of the edge off.

He settled back into his seat, leaned against the headrest and began recapping the events that brought him to this place in his life.

It all began the year before in March of 2011. The morning air was crisp. Montgomery was far enough south that winter's extreme cold was pretty much behind. He was energized and excited. This was his time of year, when serious homebuilding begins.

The foundation had been poured the week before. It was a perfect day to start framing his first project of the year, a five-thousand-square-foot

English Tudor for J. R. Dancy, a lawyer and well connected player in the state's political arena.

Clay, architect by education, designer/homebuilder by vocation worked out of his home. This suited him. He never took to the idea of punching a clock. It had been hard enough having to report eight to five during his two years apprenticeship after finishing up at Auburn University. He preferred working on his own schedule, whether it be at midnight finishing up a project or the crack of dawn, sketching out a new design he had dreamed of during the night.

He was making a comfortable living drawing house plans and building five or six custom homes per year for well-heeled clients. Life wasn't too bad, except for the sometime bouts of loneliness that typically go along with bachelorhood.

Since his divorce two years earlier, he occasionally made a stab at having some sort of social life, but his heart was never really in it. Perhaps it was too soon. He tried the bar scene, but soon realized it wasn't for him. Now and then friends fixed him up with someone they thought might be a match. Most had baggage…lots of it. He had yet to meet anyone that clicked. Friends said he was too choosy. Maybe so, but he had rather be alone than with someone just to be. Besides, being thirty-five, single with no kids and no responsibilities except for himself, there was little to complain about. He decided the best antidote for loneliness was work.

Adam got to the job site at six-thirty a.m. He was to meet Oscar Ledbetter and his framing crew there promptly at seven. It was critical to get off to a good start since the building schedule was so tight. Dancy wanted to be in his new home by the end of September; so Adam had to complete in six months what would normally take seven to eight for a house of this size with all the specified amenities.

Seven a.m. came and passed. So did seven thirty and eight o'clock… still no Ledbetter.

"Damn, a no-show," he mumbled.

This was not the first time Ledbetter had stood him up, usually lagging in two or three days later with some lame excuse as to why he didn't make it when he said he would. Usually the real reason was that some other builder had slipped him a little extra to start his job first.

"Looks like the 'Cookie Cutters' are back," he said to himself, referring to a time before the housing bubble burst four years before in 2007. Back then, houses were being thrown up, and because of easy financing, were sold even before being finished. 'Cookie Cutter' subdivisions, like weeds, were springing up everywhere. Subcontractors in all crafts were in high demand and a lot of shoddy work was going on. The great recession put an end to all of that…apparently until now.

Adam Clay was, by choice and reputation, a low-volume quality custom designer/builder, which made him pretty much recession proof. On the other hand, it put him somewhat at a disadvantage. Unlike high volume home-construction companies that built fifty to sixty houses a year, he simply could not keep a lot of subcontractors busy all the time. It had become an ongoing struggle to find and hold on to reliable, craft-oriented workmen. It was evident that Ledbetter was grazing in other, greener pastures.

Adam was about to drive off when an old faded green Ford pickup rolled up. In addition to the driver and a passenger, four Hispanic men sat in the truck bed.

"Good morning, Mr. Adam…remember me, José?"

"Hi, José," Adam responded, "I remember."

"We still look for work, Mr. Adam. Do you have anything?"

"No, not right now."

"Please, Señor, give us a try sometimes. You will not be disappointed."

José Valdez, had been coming by one of Adam's several job sites every couple of weeks for the past year trying to drum up work.

Adam never gave serious consideration to hire him and his Mexican framing crew, but was always polite with his declines.

"Have a good day, Mr. Adam," said José as he began backing his truck off the site.

"You have a good day too, José."

The truck was in the street, moving forward when Adam started waving his hands and yelled, "Wait!" He motioned for the vehicle and its passengers to come back on the lot.

The truck stopped and slowly backed to where Adam stood.

"Say I won't be disappointed."

"No, Mr. Adam, I promise. You will not be disappointed."

"I'm not easy to work for, José. I expect people to show up on time and to do first class work."

"I am the same with my men, Mr. Adam."

"When can you guys start?"

"Right now, Mr. Adam."

"I can pay $5.50 per square foot. Is that acceptable?"

"Sí, Señor. That is more than fair for us."

Adam gave José's crew a quick once-over. All were lean, wiry, and of varying skin tones and complexions. It was hard to tell, but most looked to be in their mid to late-twenties…a couple maybe in their thirties.

"OK, tell your crew to start setting up while you and I go over the plans."

José, pointed to the middle-age man sitting beside him in the cab.

"This is my uncle, Juan, Mr. Adam. He is my right hand."

José was a handsome man of about five foot-ten inches, probably in his early thirties, and obviously of Latino origin. Juan, his uncle was also nice looking but a bit weather-worn. Adam guessed that he was somewhere in his mid-forties.

Noticeably, no time was being wasted by the crew once given the go-ahead by José to set-up. This was taken as an encouraging sign.

Adam lay in bed that evening questioning his snap decision to hire José and his crew. Were the Mexicans up to the task…were they reliable…could they meet his standards of workmanship? God forbid them being a bunch of wood butchers.

Oscar Ledbetter may have been an unreliable B.S.er, but he knew what he was doing when it came to framing houses. With him and his crew, there was no need to worry about miss-alignments or out-of-plumb walls.

That was the only reason his conduct had been tolerated for the past three years. But…enough was enough. Adam Clay had had it with framers, brick masons, sheet rockers and all the others who left him hanging while they shoved other jobs in front of his. He was tired of the price gouging, being treated as if a favor was being done to take the job in the first place…and having to be grateful when they showed up in a timely manner. He knew Ledbetter would be upset. But, *too bad*, he thought, *three strikes usually means, "you're out." Let's see how the Mexicans do.*

He rolled over and went to sleep.

Chapter 2

Oscar Ledbetter and his four-man crew were at the job site when Adam arrived at seven the next morning. Ledbetter's face was red and swelled up like a bull frog.

"What's goin' on here?" he bellowed, "What are these people doin' here?"

"They're framing the house, Oscar."

"This is supposed to be my job."

"It was, but not anymore."

"What do you mean?"

Adam pointed to José and his crew who were busy at work laying the floor system: "It means these guys are going to frame this house."

"These damn Mexicans are taking our jobs," he blurted.

"No, Oscar," Adam retorted, "The Mexicans didn't take your job. You gave it to them when you didn't show up to work when you said you would."

"I had a sick baby at home, yesterday."

"That's strange, I could have sworn I saw you and your boys working over at 'Mega Homes' yesterday."

"Are you callin' me a liar?"

Adam could see that things were heading in a dangerous direction which would not be good for either of them. He knew Oscar was a hot-headed country boy who sometimes acted before thinking.

"Look, Oscar," he said, "things are the way they are. Let's just cool down and call it a day."

Ledbetter swelled even more. Just then, out of the corner of his eye, Adam saw José lay down his saw and pick up a hammer. He calmly walked over and stood behind him. A moment later the rest of the crew came streaming off the foundation and immediately stood behind José. Ledbetter's crew had been standing behind him the whole time.

"I think you better leave, Oscar," said Adam.

"Go to hell," yelled Ledbetter as he and his men got in their trucks and drove off.

"Thank you for backing me up," said Adam, "I think things were fixing to get ugly."

"Yes, we could see that, Señor," said José, "and you are most welcome."

Adam looked up at the house: "My God, You've got almost half the floor system in. What did you guys do, work all night?"

"There is little else for us to do but work, sleep and eat, Mr. Adam; so we work from the time the sun rises until darkness comes."

Adam closely inspected the work accomplished thus far. Everything was just as it should be: "Looks good, José," he said.

Five o'clock came early the next morning, but Adam decided to drag himself out of bed, get to the job site to see for himself. Sure enough, José and his crew were on the job.

"They're gone, Mr. Adams, all the two by fours are gone," were the first words out of José's mouth.

"What! All of them are gone?"

"Sí, Señor, several hundred pieces."

"That son-of-a-bitch," Adam mumbled.

He knew Ledbetter was building a house for himself up in Chilton County, but also knew that it could never be proved that he was the one who stole them. But, Adam Clay knew.

"OK, José, from now on let's mark every piece of material that comes on this site. Put my initials, AC, on everything."

It ended up being a long day for everyone.

That evening, Adam received a call from J. R. Dancy:

"Adam, it appears we've got a little problem. My wife is a distant cousin of a fella' by the name of Oscar Ledbetter. She says, he said you reneged on a contract with him to work on the house you're building for me and hired a bunch of Mexicans instead. He also said you threatened him, and ran him off the job site. What's going on?"

"J.R, first of all I didn't threaten anybody. Secondly, there was no contract between Oscar and myself. You know we're working on a tight schedule to get the house finished by September 30th; so when Oscar and his crew didn't show up when he said he would, I hired somebody else that's competent and reliable. It's as simple as that."

"Well, I don't particularly like the idea of aliens working on my house. Are they legal?"

"Frankly, I don't know. What I do know is that they are getting the job done."

"You know," said Dancy, "There's a bill going to the legislature soon that will put a stop to these illegals coming in here and taking our people's jobs."

"I don't know too much about what goes on in the political arena, but I do know that I've had a lot of problems lately relying on 'our people' to do their job. The guys working on your house are doing a good job…I'm glad to have them."

"Well, I'm not and neither are the majority of my colleagues."

"I hate that you and your buddies feel that way," said Adam, "but I don't think there are any aliens here trying to take anybody's job. I think they're here for a chance at a better life like the rest of us. And, they are willing to work hard for it. Isn't that what this country is built on…opportunity and hard work?"

"Let me get to the point, Mr. Clay. Will you call Oscar Ledbetter and take him back if he wants to come?"

"No Sir, I can't think of one good reason why I should do that."

"I can," said Dancy, those Mexicans are not only taking our jobs, they don't pay taxes, they're draining our social rescores, and…they don't vote."

First thing the next morning Adam asked: "José, do you have papers…are you here legally?"

"Why do you ask me these things, Seńor?"

"Because, I need to know."

"No, Mr. Adam, I do not have papers."

"Then, where did you get that social security number you gave me yesterday?"

"A man in Mexico got it for me"

"For a price, I suppose."

"Sí, for a very high price."

"You know I have to report what I pay you to the government based on that social security number, don't you?"

"Sí, but me and my men always pay our taxes…and social security. We ask for nothing back, except for the opportunity to work…are you going to allow us to keep working for you, Mr. Adam?"

"Yes," said Adam, "you and your men can keep working for me."

Chapter 3

It was three weeks into the job, and things were going well. Another week and the big structure should be "blacked in."

Adam liked José and was impressed by the Mexican crew's knowledge of construction. He was even learning a few tricks and shortcuts along the way that made some tasks easier.

Adam had a habit of putting a level on the floors and checking the plumb of walls every afternoon. Always, they were dead on the money plumb. To Adam's relief, José and his men maintained a neat and organized job site, which certainly was not one of Oscar Ledbetter's strong suits.

J. Roland Dancy was a brash, pretentious individual somewhere in his fifties. Physically, he was rather average. A couple of features, however, did stand out a bit. Adam mused that he probably used his beady deep-set eyes in perpetual search of opportunity and his hawk-like nose to sniff out which way political winds were blowing at the time so that he could jump on board and make himself relevant in whatever cause would benefit him the most.

J. R. visited the job site twice a week, usually on Wednesdays and Fridays. He strutted around in an arrogant manner, never speaking to or even acknowledging anyone on the crew. He spoke only to Adam. Once in a while he mumbled something under his breath in front of the Mexicans, but never spoke directly to any of them.

All in all, there was nothing he could complain about. The job was ahead of schedule, and things were being done in a good and workmanlike manner.

"Mr. Adam, we are low on nails and will need some for tomorrow," said José.

"Hmm…I have an appointment in the morning, José. Tell you what… I'll pick some up this afternoon and bring them over to your place this evening. Where do you live?"

Adam picked up a couple of boxes of #16 nails for crew's nail guns at Home Depot late that afternoon and made his way across town where row upon row of modest apartments spread the landscape.

"619…this must be it."

He knocked on the door. It almost immediately opened to a smiling José.

"Welcome to our home, Señor…come in."

The rest of the men were there, seemingly excited to have him as a guest.

There were four mattresses on the living room floor which made it apparent that the whole crew was living in the small apartment. Adam figured José and Juan had the bedroom to themselves.

"We are fixing to have supper and would like for you to join us," said José.

The air was filled with a tempting spicy aroma, and he was hungry… but Adam had a policy of not fraternizing with those who worked for him.

"Thank you, José, but I better be running along…still have work to do."

That evening, while eating his peanut butter sandwich, Adam thought of the inviting smell coming from the Mexicans' kitchen.

A couple of days later, during the course of going over some details in the house plans, José said, "Mr. Adam, my sister is to arrive from California in two weeks. She is going to start cleaning houses here. Do you think you could use her to clean your house?"

"Hmm, I doubt it José. I'm used to doing it myself."

"She is a hard worker, and you don't have to pay if you don't like the way she does."

"You should have been a salesman, José."

"She even speaks a little English," José replied.

"OK, I'll give it some thought…do you know anybody who does good trim work?"

"Sí, Señor, actually that is our specialty."

"Would you be interested in trimming this house out when the time comes? There's going to be a whole lot of crown molding in this thing."

"Of course, Señor."

The days seemed to fly by. Adam could hardly believe how smooth things were going with José and his crew. The time had come to cut them loose for a while, or at least until the brick was high enough to start construction on the back deck and screened porch. It would be a couple of months before the house would be ready for them to trim.

"Let's keep in touch," said Adam as he handed José the last paycheck for a while.

"Sure thing, Mr. Adam."

Now, it would be back to the same old headaches of dealing with subcontractors. He already had the electricians, plumbers and HVAC subs lined up to rough everything in. Fortunately, there were usually very few problems with these crafts. Sometimes, however, with brick masons, it could be another story.

Adam was the first to respect the fact that construction was hard work, especially for the likes of framers, brick masons, sheet rockers and roofers. Most of those in the trade started as kids and could never move beyond what they trained early on to do. Some developed their skills to a high level; some just got by. For some, what they lacked in education and manners, they made up for in craftsmanship and work ethic. Again, others just got by doing the least they had to. Adam tried to cut everyone as much slack as he could, but was fully aware that if he was going to stay in business he had to find the best out there. Most of the time hiring the right subs was a matter of trial and error. He had been lucky with José.

"Thank God they showed up," said Adam out loud, as the brick mason crew drove up. He didn't know any of them, but had seen some of their work. It was passable, they were available, he was desperate; so he hired them.

Like most subcontractors, Mike Hammer operated out of the bed of his truck. The thirty-something, Mike, was not a particularly likable fellow. He had an attitude and there was something shifty about him. The crew was made up of Mike, his brother, a nephew, and two helpers. Interestingly, one of the helpers, Johnny Sparrow, was a Porch Creek Indian from the reservation down around Atmore. The other was a black guy, Joe Barney, from Birmingham. Hammer, his brother, Tim, and nephew, Lee, lorded over them like they were slaves.

"Get your ass in gear and get me more brick up here, boy," or "Hurry up with that mud, Cochise," were just some of the slurs heaved upon the helpers.

Adam thought about saying something…but didn't.

Hammer and his crew worked fast. Within two weeks the brickwork was scaffold high, which was about six feet. Now, came the hard part… erecting scaffolding, a lot of climbing and much slower output. There would be two more stories to go.

Adam always paid the subcontractors on Friday. Brick masons were paid according to how many bricks they laid that week, which was based on a pre-agreed, 'price per thousand.'

Hammer showed up bright and early Friday morning, without his crew, to collect the pay check.

"Aren't you all going to set up scaffolds today?" asked Adam.

"Naw, I'm gonna' give the boys the day off. We'll set-up Monday."

Monday, came and it was a no show for the brick masons. Tuesday came and still no brick masons. About noon, Johnny Sparrow, Hammer's Indian helper showed up driving an old beat up Chevy.

"They're not coming back, Mr. Clay."

"Are you sure, Johnny?"

"Yeah, I'm sure. Mike was laughing about doin' the easy part, and bailing when we got scaffold high. It just ain't right. Me and Joe, the black guy quit."

"Thank you for coming out here to tell me, Johnny."

"Can I give you my cell phone number in case you hear of some work for a couple of good laborers?"

"Sure, Johnny. I'll do what I can."

Adam Clay racked his brain, *who in their right mind would be willing to take on a job that someone else started, especially when leaving the hard part to finish?*

That evening Adam called José:
"José, this is Adam Clay, how are things going?"
"Fine, Mr. Adam, we were able to pick up another job last week."
"That's great. I'm looking forward to getting you guys back on my job."
"Thank you for the kind words, Mr. Adam."
"José, I've got a problem. Do you by any chance know of any good brick masons?"
"Sí, Señor, I do."
"Are they really good?"
"Well, their ancestors built the Mayan pyramids down in Mexico. Sí, they are good. It is in their blood."
"Would you mind calling them and asking if they would be interested in laying brick on the house we're working on. I just need good brick layers. I've got two experienced helpers that I'll provide."
"OK, I'll call and let you know. By the way, my sister has now arrived. Have you thought anymore about having her clean your house?"
Adam looked around. *It certainly wouldn't hurt to give this place a good cleaning,* he thought.
"Sure José, when can she come?"
"This coming Saturday, if it is good for you."
"How about eight o'clock Saturday morning, then?"
"Sí, she will be there, Señor. Her name is Flor. We call her Florecita. In Spanish it means, 'Little Flower.'"

Chapter 4

Saturday morning came. It was the only day in the week he would allow himself to sleep later than six. At precisely 8 a.m. the doorbell rang. In his robe, still half asleep, holding a cup of lukewarm instant coffee, he opened the door.

"Hello, Mr. Adam. I am Florecita, the sister of José."

Not that Adam had given it much, if any thought, what he expected to see was a chubby, plain looking, dark-skinned girl like those he saw mostly in Walmart…not what stood before him.

"Hello, Florecita. I'm Adam," he stammered, "come in."

"Where should I start, Mr. Adam?"

He looked around. For the first time in a long time he noticed just how unkempt the place really was.

"Well…maybe the kitchen."

"Can I fix you breakfast?" she asked.

"No thanks, I don't usually eat breakfast, just have coffee…but feel free to fix yourself something."

"I have already eaten, but thank you."

"Well, I think I'll go take a shower and get dressed. Let me know if you need anything."

"Sí, Mr. Adam."

Adam stood in front of the mirror fixing to shave: "Jeese, what cloud did she fall out of?" he mumbled. *That face, he said in thought, amazing… wonder if she's even out of her teens?*

He began to give himself the once-over. Though having been told on more than one occasion that he was a very passable specimen of his gender, he never took it seriously, or even particularly cared. But, today that's exactly what he wanted to be...a very passable...desirable...maybe even irresistible specimen of his maleness.

He got close to the mirror and forced a grin: *Do have an OK smile, good teeth... no wrinkles yet, decent head of hair...damn...mucus in my nose...hope she didn't notice...well, except for that, maybe not too bad for thirty*-five.

He lathered up and began to shave. He wanted it smooth and close.

"Shit," *cut my lip on the first freakin' stroke...not only snot in my nose but what looks like a canker on my lip. What else can go wrong?*

With his confidence rapidly waning, he blurted again: "Who the hell are you trying to impress, Clay?" He went back into silent mode: *You're at least ten, maybe even fifteen years older than her. Shape up. She's too young... you're too old; so quit acting like a schoolboy in heat. She's here to clean your house...that's it.*

He got in the shower trying to shake his ridiculous infatuation, but the young woman three rooms over cleaning his kitchen wouldn't let him. And, now to complicate things even more, nature began to bedevil. He wanted her in there with him.

Damn you, José, why didn't you at least tell me something more about your sister other than, "She cleans real good." He let out a little chuckle and mumbled, "In case you haven't noticed, *mí amigo*, your sister looks real good, too."

After showering, drying off, combing his hair and primping a bit, he looked in the mirror one more time and checked his nostrils.

Finally, he made it through the ordeal of what should have been a simple shave and shower. Now, fully groomed and dressed, he entered the kitchen. Florecita's back was to him, scrubbing the sink. Her blue jeans fit snug, perfectly outlining a slim well-proportioned figure.

Damnit, I knew it, echoed in his mind, *the body matches the face.* So far, resistance towards being drawn to her had been a total failure.

"How are things going, Florecita," he asked.

She turned. Startled, the corners of her sensuous mouth curved downward...then, upwards into a beautiful smile.

"*Muy bien*, Mr. Adam. Did you have a nice shower?"

"Yes, thank you, it was a nice shower."

"I apologize for this place being such a mess," he said, changing the subject, "I'm at work most of the time and hadn't noticed how bad things had gotten around here."

"Don't worry, Mr. Adam. That's why you have me."

"I'm glad you're here, Florecita. Thank you for coming."

"I was just thinking, Mr. Adam," she said in a cute, quirky way of expressing in English, "if you put the glasses and dishes where the cereal and cans are, things would be much easier to get to. Do you think it is possible for me to do this."

"You arrange things the way you think they should be. It'll be OK with me."

It was good to hear her express her ideas. He liked it that she seemed to care.

"I need to go check a few job sites, Florecita. I'll be back around noon. 'Guess you noticed that there's not much to eat around here. Let me bring us some lunch. Anything special you would like to have?"

"You don't need to do that, Mr. Adam. I don't get very hungry."

"But, I want to."

"Anything will be fine," she replied.

"Tacos OK?

"Of course, I am Mexican, you know."

Adam made his usual Saturday rounds. Dancy's house was, of course, on the list, plus there were two additions and a remodeling job to check out. It seemed like a long morning. maybe longer than usual; because he was anxious to get back home…just to be around her. His admittedly foolish fantasy had him by the short hairs.

He arrived with a sack full of tacos a little after the noon hour.

"Wow," he said, you don't fool around, do you?"

"I don't understand, Señor. Have I not done well?"

"No, no, you've done great. It looks like a different place."

He walked into the kitchen…spotless. He went into the bedroom. The bed was made for the first time in months. In the bathroom all his grooming items had been neatly organized. Papers and files in the bedroom used as his home-office were orderly stacked on his desk.

"Now, I think you know more about me and the way I live than I do…pretty sad isn't it?"

"Sorry, I don't understand."

"I'm just making a little joke…let's eat before the food gets cold."

They spread things out on the breakfast room table and sat down.

She bowed her head and made a brief sign of the cross, then looked up and smiled at him. Those eyes, he thought, there was most certainly a story behind them.

"Tell me about yourself, Florecita…what part of Mexico do you come from…what made you decide to come here?"

"Well, I am from Mexico City….a very poor part on the outskirts of the city. This is paradise compared to where I come from. My brother, José heard about Alabama and came here for a better life. Now, I am here. I hope for a better life, too."

"Do you have family in Mexico?"

"Sí, My mother and sister are there."

"How old are you?"

"I am twenty-one years of age."

As they talked, Adam studied her every feature. He was struck by the symmetry of her face. One side was a mirror image of the other, forming an almost perfect oval. Perhaps this observation was the architect coming out in him. He liked symmetry. Her nose was just the right size and in the right place. Her skin was smooth with a bronze tint. Her dark hair, falling seven or eight inches below her shoulders, had a lovely sheen.

Florecita's most expressive feature was her mouth…sensuous…revealing. When those beautifully formed lips smiled, the smile was without a doubt genuine. When she was puzzled or didn't understand, it was obvious as the corners turned downwards. Adam felt that he would have no problem reading her mood, even with the sometimes spotty language differences.

Her dark almond eyes were a harder read. He wished to know what lay behind their depth. Perhaps, he thought, someday he would.

"Do you have a boyfriend back in Mexico?" he asked.

"No," she replied, "there once was a boy. He was killed in a car crash two years ago."

"I'm sorry…well…it looks like you've about finished up here. Instead of calling José, let me drive you to your place."

"It is kind of you, Mr. Adam, but I do not want to be of any trouble."

"No, no…I really would like to…and please call me Adam. Leaving off the "Mr." Makes me feel much more comfortable."

"Sí, Seńor, if you say so."

"Where do you live, Florecita?"

"I live with José and my uncle, Juan."

"Really…the last time I was over at José's place, there were four other guys packed into one small apartment. Is that where you all are living?"

"No, just before I arrived, José rented another apartment in the same building, just above that one. Now, José, Juan and I are at last together."

"That's good," said Adam.

"Yes, to me, it is a very special place. For the first time in my life, I have my own bedroom."

"It sounds like you are very close to your brother and uncle."

"Sí, my whole family is in that way."

As they rode along, Adam glanced over at Florecita. For some reason it seemed natural for her to be there beside him. He began to feel more relaxed…and less concerned about their age difference.

"Tell me about the rest of your family…those in Mexico."

"Well, my mother and sister are there. My father passed away when I was ten years of age."

"How old is your sister…your mother?"

"My sister is seventeen…my mother is fifty-five, but older than her years. Since my father died we have all had a very hard time…especially her. What about you, Mr.….aah…Adam?"

"Well, there's not too much to tell. I have no brothers or sisters. My parents divorced when I was very young. I spent my early years living sometimes with my mother and sometimes with my father until being sent to a boarding school. Both parents remarried. My mother and her husband moved to North Carolina and my father moved to Florida…he passed away last year. There's no one else except for a few distant relatives that I'm not close to. So, I'm pretty much on my own."

"That is sad. Families are very important."

"Oh, it's not too bad. I guess I'm a bit of a loner anyway."

Silence fell over the conversation.

"Say, do you like milk shakes?" he asked, restarting the conversation.

"I don't know. I have never had one."

"There's a Dairy Queen up ahead, what say we stop so you can try one?"

"You are very kind…Adam."

"Hmm, this is very good," she remarked as they sat across from each other both sipping strawberry milkshakes.

"I'll have you Americanized in no time," he said, "if you'll let me."

He looked deep into her eyes, trying to read from her what he could. She looked back into his. He wondered if this was an invitation to know her better, or was she just being gracious. He couldn't tell, but she did seem to enjoy being with him.

What he did know so far was that besides being extremely attractive she had a pleasant disposition, was humble, non-assuming and seemingly smart.

"Your English is very good…considering you just got here. You must have studied it in Mexico."

"Well, I spent a year in California cleaning houses before arriving here. That helped my English a lot. And, yes, my brother, José, insisted that my sister Maria and I learn to speak English. He made plans for many years to come to America, and it is his intention to eventually have us all here."

"That's interesting…tell me more."

"Well, José and Juan came first, about four years ago. They crossed the Rio Grande into Arizona. It was horrible. Juan almost died in the desert from heat and thirst. They only had the clothes on their back and a few dollars.

"José had heard about Alabama…that there were plenty of construction jobs, the climate was pleasant and the people were friendly and good. They finally made it here."

"José and Juan work hard. They send money home and save as much as they can so one day my mother and sister can come. It is important that our family is together. I am the first to come. Now, I will also work hard to help get my sister and mother here."

With that said, it became clear what was foremost on Florecita's mind.

"How did you get here?" he asked.

"José would not allow me to suffer what he and Juan had gone through; so he made arrangements with a man in Mexico to get me across the border and into California where I stayed in a house where other people like me were until I could come here."

As they sipped during a pause in the conversation both straws slurped at the same time. They looked at each other and laughed. Then, she gave a smile that seemed to say, 'There's much more of me to know.'

He looked at his watch: "It's after four. I better get you home."

"Thank you, Adam," she said.

Within ten minutes they pulled up to the apartment building.

"Can you come in and see our place," she asked.

"I best be on my way"…he hesitated…"Yes, I would like to see your place."

They climbed stairs to the second story, directly above the unit where José lived before with his crew. She opened the door. Instead of a barrack with mattresses strewn about on the floor, there lay a spotless, tastefully decorated living room.

"Your place looks great, Florecita, who did all this? I'll bet it wasn't José or Juan."

"No, they gave me five-hundred dollars and told to do as I wished. Now, the workers at every thrift store in town know my name."

"Well, you did an outstanding job…and on a tight budget, too."

"Adam," she said, "do you want me to come clean your house again sometimes…maybe every two or three weeks?"

"How about every week?"

Chapter 5

No doubt, Adam Clay was smitten by the young Hispanic girl who came to clean his house. Florecita was stuck in his mind…rarely leaving it. He could hardly wait until Saturday came again.

The week dragged on, most of which was spent trying to keep Dancy off his back. He was still sore about his wife's cousin being denied the framing job, and especially so because Adam was using Mexican subcontractors instead.

"You know," said Dancy, "it won't be long now until we have a law in place that will rid this state of illegals from now on. If the Federal government won't do their job, we'll do it for them."

"Well, J.R." said Adam, "I hope we can get your house built before you all's law goes into effect."

Dancy's brow furrowed accompanied by a most unpleasant frown as he turned and walked away.

Saturday morning finally rolled around. Adam got up at 5…showered, shaved, and even dashed on some after-shave lotion that had been sitting in the medicine cabinet for years. Then, he began tidying up in anticipation of Florecita's arrival.

Promptly at eight, the doorbell rang.

"Good morning, Mr…ah…Adam. I hope you had a fine week."

She was as beautiful as he remembered her to be.

"Yes, Florecita, I had a fine week…and you?"

"It was very fine. I got two more house cleaning jobs."

"I hope they aren't on Saturdays."

"No, Saturdays are for you, Adam."

He felt a rush just hearing her say that.

She looked around: "The place is as clean as I left it last week. Are you sure you need me here?"

"Of course, I need you here. I thought we'd clean out closets, today. 'Never know, we may even find some treasure in there."

A smile came to her face: "Adam, I was thinking during the week… if we moved the couch against that wall, and the chair over there, it would make the room look more balanced. Do you think it is possible to do so?"

"I never thought of it, but you're right. Let's do it."

Adam Clay was not accustomed to receiving suggestions or advice from anyone, but she had a hold on him, and he knew it. At this point, she could have probably gotten her way on just about anything.

As they pushed, tugged and rearranged furniture, he observed her every move, and took a mental snapshot of her every position. He delighted whenever she looked at him and smiled. His fantasy had now moved to another level, but he dared not let on about his hunger for her.

"There, that looks so much better does it not, Adam."

"Yes, better," he answered.

Next, came the master bedroom closet. It was a walk-in packed with things long forgotten. Frayed shirts, worn out boots, broken stereo equipment were just a few of the items headed to the dumpster.

Florecita seemed to enjoy helping rid Adam of the past. During the work-in-process she came out of the closet holding a pink bathrobe and pair of silver slippers.

"Who do these belong to?" she asked.

"He hesitated: "My ex-wife," he said, feeling a flush in his forehead and cheeks.

"You have a wife?"

"Ex-wife, Florecita. I do not have a wife, now…*comprende?*"

"What was she like?"

"She was a nice person…we just weren't made to be together."

From that point, work progressed very quietly. Adam just hoped she would not come up on anything else belonging to Susan. Then he wondered:

was she just curious about his ex-wife or a bit jealous? Twisted thinking or not, he wanted her to be jealous.

The ice finally broke when she walked out of the closet with a well-worn stuffed animal.

"Who does this belong to?" she asked.

"That's my Teddy Bear. I've had it since I was four years old. We have to keep him."

She broke out in laughter and a light-heartedness came over her, replacing the quiet somber atmosphere since discovering his ex-wife's robe and slippers.

After the closet clean-out was done, there were four full banana boxes of his past ready to be discarded. It was almost three o'clock. Time seemed to have flown by, and he was not ready to give her up for another week

"Thank you for helping me today," he said, handing over the envelope containing her pay.

"Thank you," she replied.

They stood facing each other in the living room. He looked into her dark unrevealing eyes. Then, in an unexpected impulse he held out his hands. She looked at him for a moment, and took them.

He felt heat raging through his body, wanting so much to pull her to him…to hold her…to kiss her. But, something held him back. Perhaps his subconscious was telling him it was too soon, or, more than likely it was fear of rejection.

They stood, looking at one another. He still couldn't get a reading from her eyes.

A horn honked from the driveway.

"It is José; I must go." she said.

"Next week?" he said.

"Yes, next week, she replied."

Chapter 6

I t started off being a busy week. The Mexican brick layers were hard at work and ahead of schedule. Adam had managed to get Johnny Sparrow and Joe Barney on as helpers with them. They seemed happy, were treated decently and worked every bit as hard as the Mexicans. Plumbers and electricians scurried about like in a well-choreographed dance, roughing-in utilities for the big house. Roofers clung to the steep slopes like squirrels to a tree. Adam always worried about the roofers, fearing that the day was coming when one would lose his balance and fall.

Even with all that was going on, Florecita never left his mind, and he was ever looking forward to Saturday when he could see her.

José and his crew were back sooner than expected. They were setting up to start construction on the back deck and screened porch. Adam noticed that one man was missing.

"Where's Paco?" he asked.

"He was arrested last night. He is in jail." said José.

"What happened?"

"He was driving home from the market, and the police stopped him."

"Why did they stop him?"

"They do not need a reason to stop us. It happens all the time. I, myself, was pulled over twice last week."

"Well, why did they arrest him?"

"Among the groceries was a six-pack of beer that Juan had asked him to pick up. The police accused Paco of drinking and driving."

"Well, was he?"

"No, he does not drink at all."

"And, they arrested him for that?"

"Yes, when he said it was unfair, and that he had a right to get a test to prove he was not drinking, the police became angered. They told him he had no rights, and then took him to jail."

"That's one hell of a note," said Adam, "I didn't realize things had gotten this bad for you all."

"Yes, and much worse in some cases. I'm going downtown this afternoon and try to get him out."

"Tell you what, José, let me go with you. Maybe I can help."

"That would be very kind of you, Mr. Adam."

Paco was José and Florecita's cousin. He was also Juan's nephew. Adam knew him to be a good and honest worker, a young man with a wife and two children in Mexico. He and his sister had come to the States for the same reason most of the poor, uneducated underclass did…jobs and a better life. Paco, the Valdezes and others like them hardly had a chance in their homeland to make it, and in some cases even to survive. Many of those who made it to the states, brought skills passed down from their fathers. The Valdez boy's father was a carpenter. Once here and working hard at jobs that in many cases no one else wanted, they began to see hope and even dared to dream of a better life for themselves and their families.

Adam, observed first hand that Hispanic families were very close and totally committed to one another. It was a well-known fact that those living and working here sent money back to their families in Mexico on a regular basis, including Paco.

Adam and José arrived at the police station at around two that afternoon.

"José, let me do the talking. You don't want to bring attention to yourself. They may start questioning you."

"Sí, Mr. Adam, you are right."

They approached the front desk and the officer manning it: "I'm Adam Clay. I understand you all are holding a man by the name Paco Fernando. I need to know what has to be done to get him released."

Sergeant Dunn (according to his name tag) scanned his computer screen, then said: "You can't do anything."

"What do you mean?"

"He's been turned over to the federal immigration authorities."

"Why?"

"Because he's here illegally, and he's broken the law, that's why," said the officer curtly.

"Who can we talk to regarding this?"

"Nobody here. Get an attorney if you want to take it further."

That being said, there was no choice but to leave.

Storm clouds gathered as they approached the job site.

"Let's call it a day, José. 'Looks like we're fixing to have some rough weather. I'll call my attorney to see if he can help."

Upon arriving home, Adam put in a call to his childhood friend and now attorney, Justin Walker. Justin was not available; so he left a message to call him back the next day.

Adam rarely watched TV, or for that matter kept up that much with what was going on in the world around him. But, he tuned in this afternoon, to the six o'clock news, mainly to find out about the weather.

"A bill is expected to be introduced to the state legislature in the very near future," said the anchor. "It is to be known as HB-56. According to sources, it would be the toughest immigration law in the nation, designed to rid the state of all illegal immigrants.

"Opponents to the measure say immigration is a Federal issue and states have no right to institute such a law.

"Proponents say the federal government is not doing its job; so they are going to do it for them."

"Where have I heard that before?" muttered Adam

As predicted, it was a rainy, stormy morning. Justin's call came a little after eight.

"Hey, Adam, Justin here...what's going on in your world?"

"Hi, Justin. Thanks for returning my call. 'Got a little problem regarding one of the helpers working on the Dancy house.

"Tell me about it."

"Well, a Hispanic guy by the name of Paco Fernando was arrested on trumped up charges of drinking and driving...the man doesn't drink, mind you. Now, they're sending him off to a federal immigration detention center."

"No papers, I assume."

"No, no got none."

"Well, that's more than a little problem...especially these days."

"Does he have any recourse?"

"Not much if any. Regarding the charges, who do you think the courts would believe....an illegal alien or the cops? Besides, your man is out of local and state hands if they've turned him over to the Feds."

"Yeah, I get the point."

"Adam, police departments throughout the state have an unofficial policy to hassle and make things as uncomfortable for these people as possible, and eventually clear them out of here. This comes down from higher authorities. It's a political thing. Problem is, legal Hispanics are taking the hit, too."

"You do know your buddy, J. Roland Dancy, is behind a lot of this, don't you?"

"Yeah, I do know."

"Tell you what. I'll do some checking around to see if there's any way to help this man. By the way, we're still on for our monthly happy hour aren't we?"

"Sure, I'll see you this Thursday about 5:30."

Chapter 7

Adam and Justin Walker sat in the Red Baron Lounge sharing a pitcher of draft during their monthly 'happy hour'.

"Well, like it or not," said Justin, "HB-56 (House Bill – 56) is on its way to becoming law in the state of Alabama. I guess you already know that it'll be the toughest immigration legislation in the nation, making it illegal to transport any undocumented alien, even to church. Interaction of any kind will be in violation of the law, which includes allowing them to work or even be in your home.

"Yeah, I know," said Adam.

"There'll be no hiring," Justin continued," no issuances of licenses, no social services, no protection under the law, no nothing for these people. To rent to or sell a house to any of them will be forbidden. Schools will be required to provide immigration status of enrolled children."

"Yeah, it's almost unbelievable that this can happen," said Adam. "I went to a public opinion forum the other night at St. John's Episcopal Church. Most all the churches are protesting. Hell, I can be arrested for allowing them in my vehicle, for any reason, even if it's to take them to church services. Adding to that, churches won't be able to give refuge or any kind of charitable aid to these people.

"Farmers are protesting, too. They depend on immigrants to harvest their crops, claiming that Americans refuse to work in the scorching heat, especially at the low wages they can afford to pay. Merchants are protesting, landlords are protesting…but, it's all falling on deaf ears. The politicians have a populist issue they can get their teeth into…even if it means hardship for so many, plus giving up millions in sales tax revenue for the state.

"It's Jim Crow' all over again, Justin, "They can't beat up on the blacks anymore; so they're going to pick on the little wetback guy who can't fight back. Protesters are calling this thing, 'Hate Bill – 56'."

"You're right about a lot of what you say," said Justin," and I'm sure there will be a lot of unintended consequences, but on the other side of the argument, what about those who have waited in line and done what was legally necessary to come here? One could argue…is it fair to break in line? And, there's the argument, even though I know it's being blown out of proportion, that illegals are being provided social services free gratis… stretching our recourses. And, then of course there's the old piss and moan outcry, 'They're taking our jobs.'"

"I guess it depends on whose shoes you're in on how you look at it," said Adam, "Bye the way, I think I've fallen in love with one of them."

"What!"

"She's the sister of José, head of the framing crew on Dancy's house… Paco's cousin."

"How the hell did you get involved?"

"I don't know. She's been cleaning my house…it just happened."

"I knew that you were a little crazy, Adam, but…"

"'Got any ideas on what I should do if this thing passes, Justin?"

"Yeah, maybe find yourself a nice American girl."

"No, seriously. She's who I want to be with. You know me…I don't go around falling for whoever comes along."

"Yes, I do know. That's what has me concerned, and no, I don't have any ideas. Just wait and see what happens. You never know…the courts may throw it out if it does pass. After all, immigration is supposed to be-long to the Feds., not the states. In the mean time I'll bone up on what it takes to get a 'Green Card.'"

"Thank you, Justin, I would appreciate it."

"By the way, how are you getting along with Dancy…when will you have his house finished?"

"I'm trying not to give him anything to complain about. We're ahead of schedule, thank God. I hope to be through by the end of September. "

"Watch your backside with him, Adam."

"Don't worry. I'm well aware of what that guy is all about."

Chapter 8

Finally, Saturday came…time to let go of the problems that plagued during the week. Florecita was soon to arrive. He was excited, but a little anxious. The door bell rang. He opened it, and there she was, lovely Florecita with a smile on her face…pleasant but somewhat guarded. He couldn't read her mood, but was concerned that reaching out for her hand the week before may have been too much too soon.

"Good morning, Sunshine," he said.

She broke out into a more relaxed smile: "Where should I start, Adam?"

"You know this place, now, as well as I do. You be the boss today. I'll be your helper."

"How much do you charge to be my helper?" she asked with a mischievous little smile.

"We'll talk about that later," he replied, relieved that they were seemingly in tune with each other.

While he mopped the kitchen floor as per her instructions and she dusted in the dining room, Adam called out: "You know, some flowers in the front yard would look nice. What do you think?"

"I love flowers," she said, "I think they would look delicious."

"No, flowers are pretty, not delicious."

"What is the difference?"

"Milkshakes are delicious. Flowers are pretty. You're the only thing that's both delicious and pretty."

"Oh," she said in a perplexed tone.

"I have an idea. Let's go flower shopping when we finish up here. What do you think?"

"Well, I think that is a delicious idea, Mr. Adam."

"Call José, and tell him I'll be bringing you home this afternoon."

As they rode along, heading towards Home Depot, she began to open up a little more.

"When I was a little girl I sold flowers on the streets of Mexico City. I do love flowers."

"My granddad loved flowers too," he said. "His yard had flowers for every season…tell me about Mexico City. Does it get very hot in the summer and cold in the winter?"

"It does not get too hot…about like it is here this time of year, and cold but not too cold in winter…about seven degrees."

"Not too cold…that's cold. It doesn't get any where near that here."

"Well, sometimes it is cold, especially since we only had a stove to keep us warm."

"You mean you didn't even have a heater in the house?"

"No."

"I don't see how you' all survived. Say it's about the same there as here this time of year."

"Sí, about forty degrees."

"Wait a minute, are we talking about degrees Fahrenheit or degrees Centigrade?"

"Centigrade, I think."

"Oh," he laughed, "that does make a difference. I knew Mexico was on the metric system…should have known temperature was measured in centigrade. I think I have a lot to learn about Mexico."

"And, I think I have a lot to learn about the U.S.," she replied.

"Let's make a deal. I'll teach you all about America, and you'll help me with my Spanish. I took it for two years in high school, but that's been a while back."

"OK, Spanish should be easy for you, but I don't know if it will be so easy for me to understand the ways of America, especially here in the south."

"Well you can start by saying 'ya'll' instead of 'you all' or 'all of you'."

She threw her head back: "Yaaa'll," she repeated, dragging it out in a southern drawl. She then looked at Adam and giggled. He began to giggle too, which soon turned to laughter for both of them.

He watched her eyes light up as they entered Home Depot's garden center. It was the last day of April, a perfect time to plant. There was a good selection with each flower potted in small, medium and large containers, all neatly lined up in rows and columns on knee-high platforms.

An hour later the back of Adam's Cherokee was filled with begonias, daisies, and a variety of lesser known species.

"Your yard is going to look so delicious…I mean pretty."

"Well, I know what we'll be doing next Saturday," he responded.

It was almost five o'clock.

"I'm hungry," said Adam, "are you?"

"Sí, I, too, am hungry."

"I know of a little Mexican restaurant not far from here. It supposed to be the real thing. Would you like to go there?"

"That would be nice," she replied.

"Call José so he won't worry."

"She pulled the cell phone from her purse and dialed: *"José, El Señor Adam Y yo iremos a cenar. Llegaré un poco más tarde, OK?"*

"Ok," came through the phone's speaker, *"cenaremos juntos."*

"Are you sure it will be easy for me to carry on a conversation in Spanish?" said Adam.

"Sí," she laughed, "You will see. Do not worry about saying things perfectly. "

Viva Mexico was a small family-owned restaurant, the oldest in town, specializing in authentic Mexican cuisine.

They parked, went inside, and seated themselves in the most private booth they could find.

Soft lighting cast a burnt orange color on the stucco walls and arched doorways.

"This does look like something in Mexico," Florecita remarked.

"I thought you might feel something familiar about this place," he said.

"Yes, this is like something in older parts of Mexico. But, did you know there are McDonald restaurants in Mexico," she said with a grin.

"Really."

"Sí, also Walmart, Costco and Sam's. They are all familiar in Mexico."

"I get it," he said, "They say you Mexicans are taking over here. Sounds like the Gringos have already taken over down there."

The waiter appeared, dressed in black. Two parallel gold embroidered strips donned his shirt, running from each shoulder to his waist: "Señor, Señora, my name is Pablo. I will be serving you."

"You'll have to order for the both of us," said Adam, "I get totally confused when trying to order Mexican… can't even remember the difference between enchiladas and burritos.

"Well, what does your mood call for?" she asked.

"Surprise me."

"Could I bring something to drink while you all are deciding?" asked Pablo.

"Some *horchata* would be nice," said Florecita.

"What's *horchata*?" Adam asked.

"It is a drink made from rice."

When Pablo returned with two glasses filled to the brim with a milky looking substance, she said, "I think we are ready to order, now, Pablo."

As she spouted the order mixed with a little conversation in rapid fire Spanish, Adam wondered if he could ever gain command of this language.

After ordering whatever was to come, she looked at him, smiled and said, "You will be surprised, Adam…in a pleasant way, I hope."

"You all talk so fast with each other; I don't see how anybody can understand anything."

"It is the same with me when I try to listen to a conversation in English."

As they nibbled nachos with salsa and sipped rice water, a bland but sweet and pleasant tasting mixture, while waiting to be served, he asked: "What would you like to do in the future?"

"I would like to go to school and become a teacher if I am able to stay in the states. I would like to teach little ones."

"That's a good goal, but you know it will be difficult, especially the way things are right now."

"Yes, I know."

"I would like to help, if I can."

She looked at him…in a different way than the lovely girl who had been cleaning his house. She reached across the table and placed her hand on top of his: "Thank you, Adam," she said.

A loud sizzling sound from the kitchen came closer. Then, Pablo appeared holding a tray high above his head. The platter was on fire.

"Careful, *muy caliente*," he said putting it down on the table in front of Adam and extinguishing the flame by putting a lid over the platter. Right behind him came another waiter with another sizzling, fiery platter and placed it in front of Florecita.

Pablo lit the candle on the table: "Enjoy your meal, Señor, Señora."

"This is called *fajitas carne*," said Florecita, the flame is added for effect."

They ate and talked about life and tradition in both Mexico and the states. Adam made an attempt to explain how and why the south was different from the north. Florecita tried to paint a verbal picture of the poverty ridden place from whence she came, but pointed out some of its positive aspects…mainly that of family closeness.

When finished with the meal, Adam leaned back and slapped his belly: "Delicious," he said, then held up his hand, "Pablo, please bring us two glasses of red wine…the best you have."

"Sí, Señor."

The atmosphere ripened into a romantic mood as wine was served in the soft glow and shadows of the candlelit table. It seemed to be the right time for Adam to come out with what was on his mind:

"Florecita, I don't want to wait for Saturday to come before I can see you. And, I don't want it to always be about cleaning the house. Are you interested in seeing me more…like this?"

"Yes, Adam," she replied.

An unavoidable flush came over him as the nagging question was answered in her reply. He reached across the table and took her hand. He decided to go-for-broke:

"Florecita," he said, "I think I'm falling for you."

She looked at him: "What means, 'falling for you'?"

"It means, I think I'm in love with you…no I *am* in love with you."

She looked startled. Her eyes dropped down to their clasped hands. She then raised her eyes and looked into his:

"I feel strong for you, also, Adam, but you hardly know me…and I hardly know you."

Her eyes dropped again as would a child with a case of shyness.

"I know, but I felt it in the air the first time I laid eyes on you."

They spent much of the remaining time looking at each other, smiling and sipping the wine.

It was close to nine as they approached Florecita's apartment complex.

"I hope José hasn't worried about us being this late?"

"Worried, no, he knows I am safe being with you. I believe you know that he thinks very highly of you, Adam."

Standing at the front door, he took her hand and placed the envelope in it."

"You do not have to pay me for this wonderful day," she said.

He looked into her eyes, even more deeply than before. He clasped her cheeks in his hands. She allowed his lips to meet hers. Then, he held her close…closer than he could remember holding anyone ever before. He felt her let go during the lingering kiss.

He looked again into her eyes: "My heart is yours," he said, "If you want it."

"Go slowly, Adam, I have no experience in these things."

Chapter 9

The week began with a whirlwind of minor crises...a broken water line, material shortages, ductwork routing problems...it seemed to go on and on. Finally, by Wednesday things had settled down. Though desperately wanting to see Florecita, he debated whether to call her or not. It was mid-day, she was working, he was working, and there was nothing to say other than, "I miss you." He decided that was reason enough and punched in her number:

"*Bueno,*" she answered.

"Hola, Florecita, this is Adam. How are you?"

"I am well, thank you, How are you?"

"I'm fine. 'I just wanted to tell you how much I enjoyed being with you last Saturday."

"Yes, I did too."

"I miss you," he said, "Would you like to go out for dinner this evening?"

"I can't. I have another house to clean after this one, and will not be finished until late, but thank you."

"Oh...OK, we'll go another time.

"Yes, that will be nice."

"You sound busy...we'll talk later."

"OK," she said, "goodbye."

To him, the conversation was a little abrupt, especially compared to what was usual between them. Also, there seemed to be a distance in her voice. 'Hopefully, it was just his imagination. He passed it off as that. Then, without wanting it, his mind began to churn: *Maybe I've moved too fast. Maybe she's having second thoughts regarding the feelings she expressed Saturday...got caught up in the mood...the wine. Maybe...Maybe...Maybe. Quit speculating, Clay. Be patient...things will reveal themselves, if there's anything to reveal. Saturday will come soon enough.* One thing for sure, he would not be calling her back this week.

Watching the 6 p.m. state and local news was becoming a habit, mainly because of what appeared to be a still shaky economy, and also because something was usually mentioned about the new immigration law being drafted for proposal in the legislature.

Of all people, J. Roland Dancy was being interviewed. There he was, standing in front of a camera on the Capitol's steps.

"These people have come here illegally," he orated with his usual dramatic flair. "They take our jobs, use our social services for free, their children overcrowd our schools, and most don't pay a dime in taxes…"

Adam felt the hair stand up on the back of his neck.

"Enough." He shouted.

'CLICK,' the screen went dark.

He had had enough. His mood was now so acid he was of no value to anyone, especially himself. He decided to turn in early and try to sleep it off.

Thursday came and passed without a word from her. He tried to settle himself with yesterday's thought: *Saturday will come soon enough.*

A call from Florecita came about 7:00 Friday evening:

"Adam, I will not be able to come tomorrow. My cousin, Monica, is ill, and I must care for her."

"Monica?" he said in a questioning voice.

"She is the sister of Paco."

"Is there anything I can do to help?" he asked.

"No, I will call you later."

"OK, Florecita…later."

He slammed the phone down. There would be no Saturday.

All the pent up fears of rejection came crashing down. He was bleeding from the self-inflicted wound: *What the hell was I thinking,* said his internal voice…*Should have never gotten involved. 'Should have stayed where it was safe…alone*: "There will be no more wasted emotions on something that evidently wasn't meant to be," he declared in his mental tirade.

Adam spent Saturday planting the flowers that he and Florecita bought the previous weekend. It was supposed to have been a 'together' project.

As he dug the shallow holes and examined each flower before planting it, a dreaded feeling of loss gnawed and nagged. He tried to block her out of his mind, but she would not leave. It was a long, lonely day.

Having finished planting, he went inside to shower and grab a bite to eat. It was about 4 p.m. Though there was nothing else to occupy the afternoon, he was determined not to watch the news. Perhaps he would start the book he had put off reading for the past two years. Then, he decided not to. He just sat and stared at the walls. Melancholy was rapidly turning into anger.

The phone rang about 5.00:

"Hola, Adam it is Florecita."

"Hello, Florecita."

"How are you?" she asked.

"I'm OK," he answered coolly, "how's your cousin?"

"She is better, thank you. I am sorry that I could not come today. I hope you are not angry."

"It's OK."

"Adam, if you do not have plans tomorrow afternoon, I would like for you to come dine with us. Do you think it is possible?"

His first impulse was to say, "Sorry, I'm busy," but, "Yes," came out instead, "what time?"

Despair left as quickly as it had come. Calm settled in. It appeared that the exercise in self-doubt and insecurity was all about nothing. All was well again.

Chapter 10

A little before five Sunday afternoon, Adam pulled up to the apartment shared by Florecita, her brother and uncle. He chuckled: *Well, so much for my 'never socialize with the hired help' rule*. He parked next to a bright yellow VW Beetle. "Who the hell would drive something like that," he muttered, *'Must be somebody who likes to be seen*. He climbed the steel stairs to the second level and knocked on the door. It opened with Florecita standing there with a broad smile: "Welcome Adam, I am glad you could come." She then hugged him and kissed his cheek.

Jośe, who was standing behind, stepped up: "Good to see you, Amigo," he said shaking Adam's hand, and also giving a hug.

"Thank you for the invitation," Adam responded.

"I'm sorry I could not come yesterday," said Florecita," but there was an emergency. I will tell you of it later."

"That's OK," he said, then changed the subject: "I don't know what's cooking, but it sure smells good."

"I hope you like it, Adam."

Jośe and Adam sat in the living room while Florecita trekked between the kitchen and dinning room table.

"Well," said Adam, We're ahead of schedule on Dancy's house, thanks to you guys, but it looks like the residential construction is slowing down a bit. Do you' all have enough work to keep busy?"

"Sí, Mr. Adam, there are plenty of decks and remodeling jobs. And, as you know, we are willing to take on work that others will not if it becomes necessary. We'll do fine."

"Where is Juan?" asked Adam.

"He had to go to Texas. He should return tomorrow."

Adam decided not to ask why.

"Mr. Adam, do you think the new immigration bill will pass?"

"To be honest, José, I think it will. How do folks in the Hispanic community feel about what's happening?"

"Everyone is frightened. Many have children born here, and even though they themselves came without papers they consider Alabama their home. Many fear their family will be broken up."

"I guess you know that J. R. Dancy is heavily involved in this thing."

"Sí, I know."

"What would it take for your family to get papers, Jose?"

"Go back to Mexico, apply, wait ten years and come up with at least twenty thousand dollars for each of us. We were planning to get our mother and little sister here, but now…I don't know."

"Adam glanced over at the picture perched next to a Bible on the end table: "Is that you all's mother and sister?"

"Sí, that is our mother, Margarita, and sister, Maria."

The woman in the picture must have been very pretty at one time, but it was obvious that hardships had taken their toll. The young girl; however…

"Your sister is beautiful…just like Florecita."

"Yes, she is seventeen…almost a woman."

"Supper is ready," Florecita called out.

Adam stood, observing what was around him…the furniture, pictures on the wall, the aroma in the air, the obvious aches and pains in Jose's movements, lovely Florecita bringing food from the kitchen…observing all as if adjusting his eyes to a new light.

They sat. Jose said the blessing in Spanish, then added a short plea in English: "Protect us through the storms to come. Amen." Both crossed themselves, and Florecita began serving.

"I'm not used to this kind of treat," said Adam, "It looks delicious."

Boneless chicken breast smothered in a dark gravy, reddish colored rice and re-fried beans filled the plates.

"This is a real Mexican meal," said Florecita. "Do you like?"

"Yes, very much," answered Adam after taking his first bite, "What is the gravy called?"

"Mole…it is a common part of our diet."

The discussion turned back to that of immigration, which was obviously weighing on Jośe's mind: "Our father dreamed of coming to the states. He was poor, uneducated, and knew in his heart there was no hope for a better life in Mexico. He was a carpenter, like Juan and me…could build a house with only a hand saw and hammer. He knew if he could make it to the states he could offer a better life to his family. Unfortunately, he died before fulfilling the dream. So, here we are, now, chasing the same dream."

As they finished their meal, topped off with a desert of strawberries soaked in sweet cream, Adam noticed how quiet Floriceta had become.

Looking at her, he said: "You're awfully quiet. Is every thing OK?"

She stood looking straight at Jośe: "I want him to know. Come with me, Adam."

He followed her to a back bedroom. She opened the door. Lying in bed was a plumpish Hispanic woman somewhere in her thirties. Her hair was in tangles and eyes swollen. Obviously, she had been crying.

"This is Monica, the sister of Paco. She does not speak English."

"*Monica, este es el Seńor Adam.* Adam, this is Monica."

He managed a smile and gave a little waive. She replied with the same.

"What's going on, Florecita?"

"We received a call from Paco last Wednesday. He is being held hostage by a group of coyotes. He gave them money to get him back across the border and into the states, but when he refused to bring back a pack with drugs in it, they demanded more money, One thousand dollars more. While talking with Jośe, a man took the phone from Paco and said if someone did not deliver one thousand dollars by this weekend his head would be cut off and left on the streets of Juarez. That is where Juan has gone…to deliver the money."

"My God," said Adam, "Those people are savages."

"You ask if I am OK," said Florecita. "Everything is so confused right now, I do not know what I am."

Conversation lightened between Adam, Florecita and Jośe after the unpleasant distraction. José told a story about Florecita when she was a small girl: "One day," he said, "our father brought home with him a doll for her. She was about four years of age. It was a very pretty doll with dark eyes and black hair. Floriceta loved her doll very much. She named her Lupe, after 'Our Lady of Guadalupe', the Patron Saint of Mexico.

"Not long after receiving it, the doll disappeared. Everyone looked every place they could think of, but the doll refused to be found.

"About a week later, I went up on the little hill behind our casa. A cemetery was there. It was the resting place of our grandmother. I went to plant some flowers at her gravesite.

"There, under a large cypress tree was Lupe. It seems that Florecita had gone up there and fallen asleep under the tree. When she awoke it was almost dark. Frightened that she would be in trouble, she ran down the hill, forgetting she had taken the doll with her."

They all enjoyed a good-natured laugh.

"What was Florecita like as a little girl?" Adam asked.

"She was very sweet and kind," José replied.

The evening had gone well, and with all said and done, Adam was glad he had the chance to get to know José better.

"Thank you for your hospitality," said Adam as he readied himself to leave.

"The pleasure has been mine, Mr. Adam."

"Pease call me Adam from now on, without the Mr. I'm more comfortable with that."

"As you wish…Adam."

Adam then looked at José in a most serious way: "This thing with Paco could be serious," he said, "Call if you need me…I'm serious."

"Thank you, my friend."

Florecita accompanied Adam to the outside balcony. She pointed down to the Volkswagen Beetle parked next to his jeep. Its bright yellow dominated, even in the dimly lit parking lot.

"How do you like my new car?" she asked.

He coughed and cleared his throat: "That's your car?"

"*Sí*," do you like?"

"Where and when did you get it?"

"I bought it last week from a customer whose house I clean. José helped me. I was going to surprise you with it Saturday, but… do you like it?"

"Of course. If you like, I like."

"I'm glad. I want you to be pleased."

"One thing for sure," he said everybody will know who it is when you pass by."

He leaned and kissed her lips softly: "I love you," he said.

"Adam," she said, "I feel that I, too, am falling."

"Good," he replied.

"I will definitely be there next Saturday," she said.

"Call me sometimes in the in-between times," he said.

Holding her hands in his, they looked into each other's eyes. He smiled; she smiled. He pulled her to him, and delivered a deep lingering kiss.

Then, after a long moment of each looking at the other, he said, "I best go now."

He slowly let go, then descended the steel stairs to ground level. She leaned over the balcony railing and waived as he entered his vehicle, then blew a kiss.

As he backed out of the parking space and drove away, Adam Clay felt himself entering a world he knew nothing about. But, it didn't matter…he was in love.

Chapter 11

Florecita's call came a little after eight o'clock Tuesday evening. There was great distress in her voice.

"What's wrong, Floricita?"

"Juan was too late."

"Too late…what do you mean?"

"His car broke down on the way to El Paso. He was suppose to deliver the money Sunday, but did not arrive until Monday. It was too late."

Her voice trembled as she digressed into broken English. He could hardly understand.

"Settle down Flroecita. Speak more slowly…tell me what happened."

"Can you come, Adam…is it possible?"

"Yes, I'll be right over. Did Juan get back from Texas?"

"Sí, he has just arrived."

In less than half an hour Adam was knocking on the door. Teary-eyed, Florecita opened up and immediately clung to him pressing her head to his chest. Juan was nervously pacing the floor.

"Hola, Adam. I did not expect to see you," said Jośe, rising from the cushioned living room chair.

"Florecita called," Adam responded, "what's going on?"

"I will let Juan tell you."

"Yes, I will tell you all, Mr. Adam," said Juan.

"I was to deliver $1,000 in cash by Sunday for the release of Paco. His captors instructed me to meet them at an abandoned silver mine outside El Paso, but my car broke down in Louisiana. I was not able to get to there until Monday at noon."

Juan walked to the couch where a shoe box lay. He picked it up, came to Adam and stood directly in front of him: "This is what was there…the only thing there."

He slipped the lid off the box. Adam looked down into it.

"Good God," he said.

In the bottom of the bloodstained interior lay a human finger. A wedding band was on it.

"Paco's?" he asked.

"Sí," said Juan. Paco has a wife and children in Mexico. I know it is his wedding ring because of the three little diamonds in it.

"You are dealing with animals," said Adam. "Shouldn't this have been reported to the police in El Paso?"

"Believe me when I say this to you, Señor," said Juan, "No one on this side of the border or on the other side cares what happened to Paco Fernando."

"Someone has to tell Monica," said Florecita. "I am closest to her; so I must be the one." She headed towards the back bedroom.

Within a couple of minutes, a wail came from the closed door of the bedroom, followed by muffled sobbing.

Adam watched as Juan took Paco's finger out of the box and carefully removed the ring. He laid it down on the coffee table.

"Excuse me, *por favor*," he said, "I am going outside and bury the finger."

Now, alone, José turned to Adam: "There is no need for you to become involved with the problems of our people," he said, "I apologize for Florecita disturbing your evening."

"It's too late for me not to be involved with your people, José."

"For what reason, Adam?"

"Because, I'm in love with your sister."

José gave hint of a smile: "That is no surprise, Señor. I see her also feeling in that way with you. She speaks of you all the time, and her eyes light up when your name is mentioned. I know you would be good for each other."

As he listened to José's words and tried to digest what was going on, Adam Clay, for whatever reason, thought of an old country song titled, 'Goin' Ninety Miles an Hour Down a One Way Street.'

Chapter 12

It was the last day of May, 2011. Three weeks had passed without knowing the whereabouts of Paco…whether he was alive or dead. Everyone feared for the worst, but life had to go on.

Good progress was being made on Dancy's house. José had added Johnny Sparrow and Joe Barney to his crew. He aimed to make carpenters out of them. They were both very appreciative that José had taken them under his wing. Joe, a product of foster care rearing, commented that it was the first time anyone had ever truly taken interest in him and his well-being. Things in general were going well; however a problem had developed in the budding romance which came to a head after watching an evening movie on TV at Adam's place.

"I don't understand, Florecita. You melt when I hold you. We kiss, and everything tells me you want more. Then, all of a sudden you stiffen and push away…why? What's going on?"

"I do want to be close with you, Adam…I just cannot let myself go… not yet."

"I love you, Florecita, you are everything I want. You should know that by now."

"Yes, I know…I feel the same."

"You said this is all new to you…that you have no experience. I'm trying to be patient and respectful, but know this…I need you…all of you."

She looked away and stared at the wall: "Yes, Adam, I do lack in experience, *Pero…yo no soy virgen.*"

"What are you saying, Florecita? Say what you have to say in English."

"I am no virgin," she said, her eyes filling with tears, then looking away from him.

"Well," he said, after a momentary pause, "neither am I…and that certainly is not a requirement for us to care for one another…or to be in love."

"I know there was a young man you were very close to before he was killed, and…"

"No," she interrupted, "Pablo was very traditional. He wanted to wait until we were married before knowing each other in that way."

"Then, what are you talking about, Honey?"

"When I was fifteen, selling flowers on the streets of Mexico City, a man came up to me and bought twelve red roses. He said they were for his wife. I could tell he was an important man by the way he dressed and spoke.

"The next day he came to me again and bought white daises. He said they were for the fifteenth birthday of his daughter. I thought to myself, what a lucky girl she was to have such a caring father.

"The man kept coming by, sometimes to purchase flowers, sometimes just to say, hello. I soon learned that he held a very powerful position in the government.

"One day he came by and asked me if I would be interested in cleaning his house…perhaps on a regular basis with a chance to become permanently employed as the family's housekeeper. I, of course, said, 'yes.'

"It was the best job I could ever hope for. The house was the biggest and finest I had ever seen, and in the best section of the City.

"El Señor Ortego was in his forties with a wife, two sons and a daughter my age. The wife and boys were nice enough to me, but not the daughter. She was spoiled and at times very rude with me… constantly reminding me of her position…and mine. I considered quitting because of her, but needed the job too much; so I just avoided her as much as possible. Señor Ortego had always treated me nice, like I was someone special. I thought, perhaps this was the reason his daughter treated me the way she did.

"After working there a month, coming in every Wednesday to clean, I arrived with no one there except Señor Ortego. He greeted me in an unusually warm way and insisted that I have tea with him before I began my work. I asked where his family was. He said they were all out of town… visiting relatives in another city.

"After a few sips of tea, I began to feel very drowsy."

She paused. Her eyes filled with tears again. In silence, she turned towards the wall.

"It's OK, Sweetheart," he said, "Go ahead and tell me the rest."

"It was then that he pushed me down on the couch and pulled my dress up."

Her voice trembled.

"I resisted the best I could…but was unable to scream. I was barely able to kick and swing my arms. That is when he hit me on my face so hard I almost went unconscious. All I remember after that is the pain he caused as he had his way with me. I did pass out afterward only to wake as he was on top of me again…doing the same as before.

"As I recovered, he told me how lucky I was that he found me attractive and that I was in his favor. He said he wished to continue in what he now called, 'our relationship.'

"I told him that I was going to the police. He said it would do no good, for who would believe me, a servant girl, over him…besides the police were under his jurisdiction. He then came at me again. With all the strength I had left I kicked him between his legs. As he went to his knees, I ran from that evil place."

Again, she looked away.

"Then, what?" he asked.

"My brother, José, began to tremble as I told him what had happened. Juan put his hand on his shaking wrist and said, 'Calm yourself, Nephew. Together, we will take care of this matter.'

"A week later, El Señor Ortego was found in an alley with his throat slit. Everyone, including the authorities, concluded that the deed had been carried out by one of the drug cartels that it was rumored he was connected to. Nothing was ever mentioned in our family about the incident."

Her eyes fell to the floor: "Now you know," she said. "Probably I am not fit for anyone."

"Don't say that, Florecita. You are more than I have ever even dreamed of. You are who I want to share my life with. What happened to you is terrible. And, I do understand how you must feel, but life goes on. I love you, Florecita, even more, now, and nothing is going to change that."

"Thank You, Adam…I love you too."

He held her close.

Several moments passed: "Forgive me, Adam," she said, "but, I feel the need to go for now. I hope you will not be too angry with me, but there is a lot for both of us to think about."

"Ok," he replied, "I understand."

"Adam, I am so sorry to cause you displeasure. I hope you will not stay angry with me too long."

"I'm not angry, Florecita…we'll work through it."

"He walked her outside to her VW Beetle, gave a brief kiss, and watched her drive away.

He paced the floor. There was such restlessness inside, there was no way he could concentrate on anything. Darkness fell: "I've gotta' get out of here," he mumbled.

Chapter 13

It was close to nine o'clock as Adam cruised the downtown streets of Montgomery. Like most southern towns there was very little activity during the week at this time of night, even in the state's capitol. The capitol building loomed on a hill at the end of Dexter Avenue, lit with floodlights that gave shadowy outlines of statues and monuments. It was as if they were giving dark testimony of Alabama's history of defiance and sometimes violent resistance to change.

Emotionally on the fence regarding the latest situation with Florecita, he felt the need to escape…at least temporarily. Temporarily, because he knew she would not…and most likely never would leave his mind. Then he rationalized…*life wouldn't be life without problems.*

After driving a while longer, his mind drifting, he found himself pulling into the parking lot of the Red Baron Lounge where he and Justin would meet for their monthly happy-hour.

Since it was during the week and a little late for most of the regulars, the place wasn't crowded…no more than twenty patrons…and there was no band. *Thank God for that*, he thought.

Adam took a seat at the bar. Stools on either side of him were vacant.

"What'll you have?" asked the bartender.

"Gin and tonic with lime," he replied. This was his 'reflective drink'… when he drank, which wasn't often. It was light and forgiving with no after taste…good company to sip on and think.

He looked around the room…not too big, but big enough…dark but enough light to tell what was going on…a decent place to sit awhile. It was fairly easy to profile those who were there…and why they were there. At one end of the bar two men in suits, both with shirt collars unbuttoned, and ties loosened, were engaged in robust conversation…most likely out-of-town salesmen telling war stories. At one of the tables across the room, about twenty feet away, sat a couple being much too intimate to be legitimate. Then, there were a couple of guys milling around with drinks in their hands...*hunters, cruising for prey.*

He turned back around and rested his forearms on the padded bar ledge. There was a mirrored wall behind the bartender's work area with bottles of different liquors neatly lined up in front of it on a counter. He looked at his reflection. *You look a little lonely fella'*, said an inner voice.

He watched himself sip his gin and tonic while trying to decide whether to think through the problems at hand or just relax and let the spirits take him where they willed.

He saw the reflection of someone coming from behind, then taking a seat on the bar stool to the right of him. She was blonde. What he saw in his peripheral vision made him curious enough to take a quick glance.

"Hi," he said, slightly raising his glass.

"Hi, yourself," she said...a subtle gravel in her voice. "I'll have my usual, Tony Baby," she said to the bartender.

"One vodka-collins comin' up."

She looked over at Adam: " 'Haven't seen you in here before."

"Well, I don't get out much...do you come here often?"

"About once a week...just to get out for a while."

"Are you from here?"

"No...Hattiesburg, Mississippi...what about you?"

"Yes, except for college, I've lived here all my life...I'm Adam Clay, " he said, extending his hand.

"I'm Wanda...pleased to meet you."

She appeared to be somewhere in her mid-thirties...blonde, slim with well-defined features and cherry-red lips...maybe a little weatherworn, but she looked good...at least in the low light.

"How long have you been in Montgomery, Wanda?"

"Goin' on five years. I came here after my divorce to work at a trucking company. I've been dispatching big rigs ever since. What do you do?"

"I build houses."

"That's interesting. I've always wanted a tree house...'think you could handle that?"

"Probably so."

The conversation continued…light, flirty and pleasant. Two drinks was his limit when driving, but he was now ordering his third gin and tonic as well as a second vodka-collins for her.

Somebody fed the jukebox. An old country classic from the '70's called, 'Help Me Make It Through The Night' came on. It was sung by a once upon a time songbird named Sammie Smith.

"How 'bout a dance, Handsome," she said.

"I'm pretty rusty, but I'll try."

As they slow danced she ran her fingers through his hair and pressed her cheek to his. He held her close with one hand pressing her back…the other much lower, pressing even more. He was feeling his drink.

As they danced their heads turned to each other. She looked at him… he looked at her. Her lips came to his, then his to hers. And, they danced.

As the song was ending, she whispered: "Let's go to my place. It's not far from here."

He squeezed her hand as they headed back towards the bar. He looked at his watch. It was approaching eleven o'clock.

"Thank you for the invite, but I really need to go. My day has to start early tomorrow…some other time, maybe?"

"Sure," she said.

He paid for both his and her drinks, gave her a brief kiss, then, with parting words, "It was nice to meet you," he headed for the door.

"Sure," she called out.

After turning down what he probably would have later regretted, he steered towards home.

Twenty minutes later: "What the hell," he said aloud as he drove up to the house. Florecita's VW was parked in the driveway. He pulled up behind the yellow bug, exited his vehicle and his made way towards the front door.

He entered the darkened living room. She was on the couch, asleep in a sitting position; her head slumped to the side. A soft purr came from her breathing. He touched her cheek

"Florecita," he said in a soft voice.

Her eyes slowly opened:

"Hello, Adam,"

"You decided to come back," he said, "I'm glad."

He leaned over and put his lips to hers. She gave a gentle response, and looked up at him with her dark almond eyes:

"I am here for you, Adam…anyway you will have me."

"I love you, Florecita." With that said, he took her hand, gave a slight tug as she rose from the couch. He led her to the bedroom.

Chapter 14

They stood next to the bed facing each other. The only light was that coming from the bathroom. He pulled her close…kissed her, and began unbuttoning her blouse. Half way done, he felt her tense up. *Not too fast,* warned his inner voice. He stopped, clasped her face in his hands and gently kissed her again: "It's OK," he said in almost a whisper.

He began unbuttoning his own shirt, took it off and let it fall to the floor. He then unbuckled his Dockers and slipped out of them. Next, came the briefs. She said nothing as he stood naked before her, and looked nowhere but into his eyes as he took her hand and first rubbed it against his bare chest, his stomach, and then further down. She made an instinctive attempt to jerk her hand back, but he held it there.

"It's OK," he said, again.

After a few moments she seemed to settle some. He continued unbuttoning her blouse, then slipped it off allowing it to join his clothes on the floor. He pulled her to him, reached around and unhooked her bra. It fell forward. She let it slip off her arms exposing her breasts in the shadowy light emitting from the bathroom. He pulled her to him again until her breasts pressed firmly to his chest. He began a slow gyrating motion. He felt her relax as she started to move in rhythm with him.

The time had come. He unbuttoned her jeans and in a smooth single movement pulled them along with her panties to the floor. She stepped out of them.

He guided her to the bed and laid her down. On her back, she crossed her legs, folded her hands and rested them on her stomach. With his vision now adjusted to the low level light, he stood and gazed down on her. The unveiled beauty before him was even more desirable than he had imagined. With all senses heightened, he laid himself down beside her.

Finally, they were face to face, skin to skin…just a heartbeat from one another. His fingertips traced her lips, her nose, her ears, then drifted downward. She responded with deep approving sighs. She was letting go.

He felt her heart race as he kissed between her breasts and worked his way downward, savoring every inch of her smooth taut skin. Her stomach pulsated as she breathed.

He paused at her navel and kissed the sensuous shallow well as a flood of wetness came from under his tongue. He then moved downwards towards the final destination. There, he did what he knew to do.

Her body began to twitch and writhe. She arched her back: "*Ven*," she shouted.

He positioned himself, then raised her legs. He looked down on her, taking in all he could. Their eyes locked as he entered his fantasy.

Someone, somewhere along the way said, 'Never say, *I love you*, while making love for the first time.'

He said it anyway: "I love you, Florecita. I love you more than I can ever say."

From parted lips she whispered: "*Tu ares mi amor…mi corizón.*"

They made love throughout the night, lost in a world they had made for themselves.

He stood watching her in the early morning light. Her hair spread out over the pillow. Her arms cradled above her head. To him, she truly was a Sleeping Beauty.

He leaned over and lightly kissed her cheek, then slipped into his robe and headed towards the kitchen. As he put on a pot of coffee, his mind began to replay the events that led to this moment. He questioned…how could it be, the one-in-a-million chance of them ever meeting, and now, the improbability of this? How could it be, he wondered.

He went back to the bedroom. She lay there; her eyes open, staring at the ceiling.

"Good morning," he said.

Her dark eyes cut to him: "*Buenos dias, mi Amor.*"

"Are you OK?" he asked.

"*Sí,* and you?"

"I'm fine…no…I'm perfect." He kissed her, and ran his hand over her raven hair: "Ready for coffee?"

"*Sí*, but I only have the clothes I came here in."

He went to the closet, and soon returned with a shirt…one of his favorites because the tail was extra-long. "Here, this should do."

He watched with intense delight as she slipped out of bed, and stood there for a moment in her full naked beauty examining the shirt before putting it on.

He knew it was innocent taunting as she sat across from him on the couch with her smooth bare legs so exposed, and the shirt only half buttoned, but it caused him to want more.

As they sipped morning coffee, he wondered if he would ever be able to get enough of her.

"Are you hungry?" he asked.

"Not too much, but I would like to wash."

"Can we shower together?" he asked, "I would like to."

"*Sí*, we can shower together if you wish."

As he lathered her back and shoulders, he remembered something from the first time she was there. He turned her around. As they faced each other the warm water fell like a summer shower, streaming through their hair, over their faces and down their bodies forming droplets along the way.

"I have a confession to make," he said.

"What you mean?" she asked.

"I fantasized about taking a shower with you the first day you came here."

"Adam, you silly man. You did not even know me then."

He pulled her close. They kissed only as new lovers can.

"I do now," he said.

Chapter 15

In the days that followed, when not at her job cleaning houses, Florecita was mostly either with Adam or at his place, cleaning, tidying and putting her own touch on things.

Over dinner at Viva Mexico, which had become their favorite restaurant and rendezvous, Adam directed the conversation to serious upcoming matters.

It was June 8th, the eve of HB-56 becoming law in the state of Alabama.

"You know, Florecita, as of tomorrow it will be illegal for you to work cleaning houses. Have you discussed this with your clients?"

"No, I do not think that they are even aware of it."

"Well, they will be…in short order."

"What should I do, Adam?"

"Quit…quit all of them, immediately."

"I can't leave my customers like that…they depend on me."

"I'm afraid you'll have to. If you're reported, it could be serious."

"But, I have to work."

He gazed across the table at her in a stern and determined manner.

"No you don't. You don't have to work, period. I want you to be with me…all the time."

"All the time?" she said.

"Yes, I want you to move in with me. I want you to marry me. I know it's soon…maybe too soon, but that's what I want…more than anything else in this world."

She cocked her head and gave a puzzled look: "I do not know what to say."

"Just say, yes."

She leaned a little forward. Her eyes became deep dark wells that began to overflow.

"Yes, *Mi Amor*, if that is what you want, it is what I want."

He reached across the table and put her hands in his. He smiled: "I love you," he said.

"I love you, too," came like a warm southern breeze from her perfectly formed lips.

"How do you think your brothers will feel about it?" he asked.

"They are very protective of me, as you know. But, I am now a grown woman and must make my own decisions. I do know that they think highly of you, Adam, and I know they want me to be happy...I know they will be pleased."

There wasn't much to bring...just her clothes, some personal items and a few photographs. After settling in, it felt natural...as if she had been there all along. She had no problem taking charge of the details of running a household. In Adams view, she was borderline fanatic when it came to cleanliness and order. But, he reveled in the attention she gave him.

"I never thought I could feel this way," said Adam to Justin Walker during their monthly afternoon get-together at the Red Baron Lounge.

"I'm happy for you, Adam...but be aware of the problems facing you and Florecita. This HB-56 thing is now law, and the political wolves are out for raw meat...as in Hispanics. Most of the population is either confused or too scared to do or say anything about it. Even the churches are now afraid to transport any Hispanics, documented or not. You are aware, Adam, aren't you, that you could go to jail for harboring one?"

"Yes, I know," was Adam's only reply.

June passed into July without incident. They planned to marry in the fall, after finishing Dancy's house. It would be a good time to take a break. Perhaps they could drive to Savannah Georgia, head south hugging the Atlantic coast through Florida all the way to the Keys, then come back up the gulf coast to Mobile.

It was a trip he had always wanted to take, but with Florecita at his side, as his bride, it would be a dream honeymoon.

One Friday Adam came home early from the job: "Florecita," he said, "It's been a rough week. I need a little break…a change of scenery. Why don't we go down to Gulf Shores for the weekend? I know you'll love the beach, and it's just a three-hour drive from here."

She, of course, was on board with whatever her Adam wanted to do.

The next afternoon Adam and Florecita stood at the front desk of the 'Beach-Side Resort' Hotel…checking in.

The young clerk quickly shifted his eyes from Adam to Florecita, then back to Adam: "Sir," he said, I've been instructed to ask for an I.D., if…" The clerk paused.

"If what?" said Adam, feeling a flush come to his face and forehead.

"Well, if someone seems like they may be…" He paused again.

"What, illegals?" Adam interrupted, "Hispanics, wetbacks?"

"Yes, Sir."

'Malcolm', was imprinted on the name tag of the young man who happened to be African American.

"Malcolm," said Adam, "You're treating us like your granddaddy would have been treated back in his day, sixty years ago. Now, why don't you take my credit card, register us and give me the key, or whatever's used these days to open the door…OK?"

"Yes, Sir," he replied. Then, without further discussion he registered them and handed Adam the card that would open the door:

"You know, I'm just trying to do my job, Mr. Clay."

"Yes, I know, Malcolm."

"Maybe you should complain to the lawmakers of this state," retorted the clerk, "not people like me. They're the ones causing all of the problems…and while you're at it let them know that we've lost most of our cleaning staff because of them."

"I may just do that, Malcolm."

Their fifth floor room was large, clean and well appointed, with a king-size bed strategically placed so as to take advantage of the gulf breeze if the sliding glass doors were opened. The view was spectacular from the small private balcony. With the pure white sugar-sand beach below and constant sound of waves pounding the shore, it seemed to be just what was needed to calm Adam.

The sun was setting. Its red-orange colors spread across the horizon, just above the western waters: "Honey, I hope you're hungry for some seafood," said Adam, "I've been thinking about it all day."

The restaurant had a down-home 'fifties' feel. Though packed, the atmosphere was pleasant, and the waitress friendly.

Adam ordered their largest seafood platter, and talked Florecita into doing the same.

"Adam, I cannot eat all of this."

"I know. That's why I wanted you to order it: so I can finish off what you don't eat."

After feasting on what was without a doubt some of the best seafood anywhere, they drove the busy parkway that was lined with high-rise condos, hotels, motels, souvenir stores, and nightspots. They arrived at their hotel room about 8:30. Adam walked out on the balcony. The full moon shimmered on the water and illuminated the foamy waves as they broke on the beach. He saw no one walking the shoreline.

"Honey," he called to Florecita who was in the room unpacking, "Do you feel like taking a walk on the beach?"

"Yes…I would like to."

Within fifteen minutes, after changing into their bathing suits, they were on the deserted beach, taking an evening stroll …walking, talking, holding hands, their bare feet imprinting the soft sand with every step. Small waves lapped the shore, inviting them to come in and enjoy the gulf's warm waters.

"Let's go skinny dipping," he said.

"What means skinny dipping?"

"Come, I'll show you."

He took her hand and they made their way into waist deep water. There, he held her to him while reaching behind and pulling the bow knot that held up the top part of her bathing suit. It fell on the calm water exposing her upper body. The top floated as he tugged at the bottom part getting it to her ankles. She stepped out it, leaving her completely naked.

As she reached down into the water to retrieve the bottom part a big wave came in, jostling them helplessly about for several seconds.

"Adam," she cried, "They are gone…my clothes are gone."

In near panic they searched all around, but indeed they were gone. All of Florecita's two piece bathing suit had been washed away…taken by the thieving gulf.

Resigned to that fact, Adam said, "Let's make a run for the hotel."

"What means that," she asked.

"Never mind, just stay close behind me."

What was a deserted beach now became populated with couples, some with kids, walking the shore line.

They ran in the light of a full moon, him holding her hand and keeping her as close behind him as possible. As they passed a family of stunned onlookers, the mother grabbed her kid and unsuccessfully tried to cover his eyes. Adam briefly looked up at the hotel. Someone in a small group was pointing at them from one of the upper floor balconies.

They came to some azalea bushes that were a part of the hotel's landscaping.

"Stay here," he said, "I'll be right back."

Thank God I didn't get my trunks off before the wave hit, he said in silence as he entered the hotel lobby.

"Malcolm, I need a big towel, quick. I'll explain later."

Malcolm went to the back, and moments later came with a towel, not that big, but it was better than nothing.

"Thanks," he said, then rushed back to the bushes where Florecita was waiting, teary eyed.

As they scurried through the lobby towards the elevator with Florecita's bottom exposed because the towel wasn't big enough to completely cover her, Malcolm stood behind the front desk with his mouth open. Several hotel guests just stood and stared.

Adam, looked over at him, smiled and winked: "Wetbacks," he said.

After laughing off the incident and showering, they laid down to rest on the king-size bed. With the fifth floor sliding glass doors open, a gulf breeze gave constant caress to their bodies as they lay there on their backs, naked, holding hands. He turned his head and looked over at her. She looked at him. He smiled. She smiled back as always. Then, they made love as the warm gulf breeze bathed them.

With the hypnotic sound of waves, and the love of his life beside him, life could not have been better at that moment for Adam Clay. It had been a long time since he had truly been at peace with himself and the world.

Thank you, God, he uttered in solemn thought before drifting into sleep.

The next day, all day, was spent on the beach…in the water…out of the water…lying on towels, sunning…walking east…walking west…people watching…back in the water…out of the water and on and on.

As the sun began to set, Adam looked at Florecita: "It doesn't take much sun for you, does it? I'm gonna' start calling you, 'My Little Brown Berry'."

"Well, Mr. Adam, you just may end up with two little brown berries before too long."

"What do you mean, Honey?"

"My time of the month has not come since we first made love."

Chapter 16

The revelation of Florecita's pregnancy changed everything. On the drive back from their weekend getaway, Adam turned to her:

"Florecita, we can't wait until fall. We need to marry, now."

"Yes, I know, *mi Amore.*"

As they drove, Adam's mind drifted. Once again he thought about how fate had intervened in his mostly solitary life. He wondered about the odds of connecting with the young woman beside him who was not only four-teen years his junior, but from a totally different culture some two thousand miles away. Was it just dumb luck or something else? Could it be that that it was meant to be all along… but had to wait until the love of his life was ready for him… until the gap of age and miles closed. Either way, now, at last, she was with him. And, she was going to have his baby.

The next morning, after making rounds at the Job sites, he and his bride-to-be were in line at the Montgomery County Court House to procure a marriage license.

"I need you'alls I.D.s," said the heavy-set woman behind the counter in a business-like manner.

Adam and Florecita presented their drivers' licenses.

The woman looked at Florecita: "I need to see documentation regard-ing your status here in this country, ma'am."

"I have no such papers," said Florecita before Adam had a chance to say anything.

"I'm sorry; I can't issue a marriage license without proof of your legal status, Miss Valdez."

"Wait a minute," said Adam, my lawyer and I are working on her status. We just want to get married without a hassle. Can't you help us with this?"

"No, sir, the new law says, no licenses will be issued without evidence of legal status…by the way, Miss. Valdez, without documentation your driver's license is no longer valid."

Adam said nothing more. He took Florecita's hand, they turned and walked away. He knew that he couldn't afford to make a scene, nor did he want anyone to see the boiling rage inside.

That evening, he decided to go on the internet and for the first time take an in-depth look at HB-56, now referred to by many as, Hate Bill – 56.

As its venom spewed from the computer screen, it soon became clear that this law was designed to make life miserable for the un-documented. Its intension was not only to run every one of them, namely Hispanics, out of Alabama, but also to uncaringly wreck lives in ways only Jim Crowe could have come up with. Adam felt a weakening nausea as he continued to read the hatefully crafted words that had somehow become law.

Not that he was learning anything he didn't already know, but reading it letter by letter, word by word , somehow brought it all home.

Nausea turned to anger:

Who the hell do they think they are, telling me who I can and can't associate with… have in my car, my home…who I can and can't love…marry. What god forsaken government or law has these rights? This is America, not Nazi Germany.

He picked up the phone and dialed:

"Justin. Adam, here," he said, leaving a message on the answering machine, 'I need to set up a meeting with you as soon as possible…as my attorney."

"Frankly, I don't give a damn about what's right, wrong, justified, legal or not," said Adam in his meeting with Justin the next day, "I'm in the shoes I'm in, and that's what matters to me. What can I do to protect Florecita… and myself?"

"Adam, there's nothing you can do for the moment, but, now, everybody's seeing that this thing is loaded with unintended consequences.

"Apartment and mobile park owners are raising hell. They can't rent to anyone even suspected of being undocumented. Tomato farmers all over

Alabama are left with crops rotting in the fields. Since all the immigrant workers left, they can't find anybody willing to get out there and deal with the heat. Churches are afraid to transport Hispanics or even allow them into services. Schools claim they're bogging down in paper work processing and reporting undocumented children. Even the cops are complaining saying that they have more urgent matters to be concerned with than chasing down undocumented aliens."

"Well, things can't go on like this," said Adam. "Is anybody trying to do something about it?"

"There's a lot of legal minds, including the Feds looking at this thing. All opinions I've heard so far is that it's as unconstitutional as hell. Law suits are being filed as we speak. Just lay low for now, Adam. I think in time, things will change."

"I don't have time, Justin, she's pregnant."

"Adam, lay low for now."

Chapter 17

Adam took Justin's advice. He and Florecita settled in as a couple living a low profile lifestyle. She no longer cleaned houses, but sometimes accompanied Adam to job sites just so that they could be together.

They grocery shopped mostly at Walmart where, now, there was a noticeable absence of Hispanics. Adam had heard estimates that the state would lose at least five million dollars in sales tax revenue during the year due to the exodus of immigrants.

Every night on the local news there was something mentioned regarding the impact of HB-56…news of crops going unharvested, shortages of labor for cleaning, restaurant and outdoor work, apartment vacancies, suits being filed challenging the constitutionality of the law, and on and on.

One news report in particular got Adam's attention. A woman in north Alabama threatened to shoot the governor because of being denied a marriage permit. Her husband-to-be was an undocumented Hispanic.

It was mid-August. The call came during supper:

"Señor Adam, this is Paco. Can you talk?"

"Paco!" replied Adam, "yes, of course I can talk. Are you Okay?"

"Sí, Señor, I am Okay."

"Where have you been for the last three months? We thought you were dead."

"Things are very different for me, now, Señor. I will have to explain later, but today I need to ask something of you."

"What do you need, Paco?"

"I need you to meet me in Birmingham this weekend and pick something up for Juan and my sister, Teresa."

"Why don't you just come home? Your sister and cousins have grieved a long time over losing you. Don't you think you owe them an explanation?"

"It is complicated. Can you do what I ask?"

"Alright, Paco, When and where?"

While hitting the disconnect on his cell phone, he looked up. Flore's eyes were as wide as he had ever seen them, "Paco, my cousin?" she blurted.

"Yes…he wants me to meet him Saturday night at some Hispanic night spot up in Birmingham."

"How could he do this to us?" she said, tears welling in her eyes, "not even letting us know he is alive…after all the tears we have shed over him…especially Teresa."

"I don't know," Adam replied, "Do you want to go with me?"

"Of course, I want to go."

As darkness fell that Friday, Adam and Florecita began the two-hour drive north on I-65 to Birmingham. They were to meet Paco at nine o'clock. The place was called 'La Luna.'

There was little discussion along the way in that both seemed to be lost in their own thoughts regarding what was going on. Time passed fast and before either expected they were entering the parking lot of 'La Luna'. Adam looked at his watch. It was 8:55.

The freestanding building was large, completely lit with red, blue and green lights flashing on its exterior. Fifteen-foot fake palm trees lit by neon scattered in the parking lot providing light there.

Outside, at least a dozen young girls, some Hispanic, some obviously Gringa mingled among twice that many Hispanic males. All the females were dressed in skintight short shorts and exposing halter tops that left little to the imagination. The girls looked to be very young…many were overweight.

A rough looking middle-aged Hispanic man stood at the entry, behind what looked like a church pulpit and collected a ten-dollar cover charge.

"There's two of us," said Adam as he handed the guy a twenty. The man looked at him without smiling and with obvious suspicion as he rubber-stamped the top of both his and Florecita's hands.

Entering, they crossed the threshold into another world. The inside seemed even larger than the outside. Ear shattering, bass pounding Latin music came from a far corner where the dance floor was located. The middle section was dedicated to a maze of tended bars that snaked from front to back. The place smelled of spilt beer and cigarette smoke. To the right there a full-size wrestling ring. Folding chairs backing up to the ropes lined the entire interior parameter of the ring. In the chairs, about twenty in all, set young Hispanic men waiting their turn for a lap dance performed by one of the three half-naked women making their way around the ring. Folding chairs were outside the ring where drinking spectators waiting their turn cheered and blurted catcalls. It was as if Juárez, the Mexican border-town just across the Rio Grande from El Paso were right here in the heart of Dixie.

Adam wondered how this bunch had escaped the purge. Evidently, HB-56 was exempt in this place. He had been in his share of seedy night-spots. This was close to the top on a scale of one to ten.

He looked at Florecita, "Are you OK?"

"Yes," she replied.

"Paco said to go to the back where there were tables and it was quieter. He said he would find us."

Many of the patrons, mainly young men, just stood around, sipping on their can or bottle of beer while quietly observing everything going on. Every eye was on Adam and Florecita as they made their way toward the back. There was no doubt that they were the aliens in this land.

It was relatively quiet and private in the far back where the tables were. They sat across from one another. He reached out and took her hand: "Thank you for coming with me."

She smiled: "*Denada*."

Soon, a man approached carrying a briefcase. Adam did not recognize him.

"Señor Adam," said the man. It is me, "Paco."

Adam immediately looked down at the man's left hand. His ring finger was gone.

The once clean cut Paco now had a mustache and goatee. He looked older … sinister …not a trace of boyish innocence left.

"Is it really you, Paco?" said Florecita

"*Sí, Bonita Nina*, it is me."

She jumped up, hugged him, clung to him and cried, "Why have you done this to us?"

Adam interrupted: "*Oue Passa*, Paco, what's going on?" he said in a stern, no nonsense voice.

"I needed you to come for this," he said placing the brief case on top of the table. He then opened it. Inside, neatly stacked, were hundreds of twenty-dollar bills.

"What do you want me to do with this," asked Adam looking hard into the eyes of the man he once knew as among the most gentle of souls.

"I need you to take this to José. It is for him to take care of my sister, Teresa. I will not be able to help her in any other way."

"The first question I have for you, Paco, is why are you not delivering this yourself?"

"I cannot risk putting the family in danger, not only by the authorities, but by others. I should not be in direct contact with any of them living here in the states."

"Well, what about Florecita and me."

"You are safe. They would not dare draw attention to themselves by bringing harm to an American outside the cartel."

"So," said Adam, "you've gone to the dark side."

"I was given no choice, *Amigo*. It meant my wife and children in Mexico, my uncles José and Juan here the states, my sister, and yes, even you, Florecita."

"Tell me…tell me everything that's happened since the time you disappeared until now."

"I was being held prisoner by three hombres…supposed reliable coyotes. One was called Jefe, or Boss. When Juan failed to show up with ransom money, Jefe told the other two to hold me down. He took a chisel and hammer and chopped off my finger. He said it would be left there along with my wedding band as a reminder to Juan to be respectful to time when he had an important appointment. He said not to worry, though. If Juan did not come, my finger would not go to waste…it would be eaten by rats.

"As I suffered the pain of losing my finger I was told that since I knew Alabama I was to become a runner from El Paso to Birmingham and Atlanta.

"I told him that this was not something I wanted to do; so to go ahead and kill me. Jefe said, 'No, we will simply start with your family in Mexico…one by one.'"

"So, señor, Adam, here I am."

"How much money is here, asked Adam?"

"Twenty thousand dollars, *Señor*."

"I will take it this one time," said Adam, "but do not call any of us again until you are free of this."

"There is only one way to be free of this, Senor."

"Then, live high while you can, my friend."

"*Si*…I will escort you all out to the parking lot."

It was a long drive back to Montgomery. Little was said along the way.

Chapter 18

August gave way to September without any major incidents. Florecita was in her fourth month. Except for an occasional bout with morning sickness, she was full of energy, restless and anxious to do something physical.

"Adam, who cleans your houses after you have finished them?"

"I usually hire a crew that specializes in cleaning newly constructed homes."

"Do you think it is possible that I can have that job?"

"Honey, you're four months pregnant, and there's a lot of hard work involved. It's not just a matter of vacuuming, dusting and polishing…there's windows to be scraped and cleaned, a great deal of down-on-your-knees scrubbing and sometimes heavy lifting."

"I know I can do it, Adam. You know how hard I work, and my cousin Teresa will help. She also works hard and is in need of a job."

"Well, it's against my better judgment, but I am about to finish up Dancy's house. Go ahead and give it a try if you want to, but if it doesn't work out I'll have to get somebody else. Don't get your feelings hurt if that happens."

A smile came across her face: "You do not have to worry, Adam, that will not happen…you will see."

Knowing his Florecita as he did by then, Adam was not surprised that she and Teresa proved to be a crackerjack team…thorough and fast. By the end of the week they were wrapping things up on the Dancy house. Then, at the dinner table, Florecita announced: "Mrs. Dancy has been coming by every day. She is a very nice lady."

Adam looked up from his plate: "I wish I could say the same for her husband."

"She wants me to come and work for her."

"What?"

"Mrs. Dancy wants me to help her move and organize things. She likes my ideas on decorating, too."

"Florecita, don't you realize that her husband, J.R. Dancy, is one of the ones behind the HB-56 immigration bill. They want to kick all Hispanics out of Alabama. That includes you, Honey."

"It will be part-time and only last for a couple of months. Please allow me to try. I do like the lady and love the house you built. I would like to put my touch on it."

"You know I won't say, 'no'. Just be aware that J.R. Dancy is no friend of your people.

Personally, I'm glad to be rid of him."

Ironic, thought Adam, that Dancy would allow his wife to bring an 'Undocumented' anywhere close to his house.

"How did she get J.R. to agree to this?" he asked.

"She told him that she could not find anyone else without it costing a lot of money."

That hypocritical S.O.B., streaked through his mind. Here was a man now violating the very law he championed. He had known his share of 'Dancys' who always had a self-serving agenda, and applied double standards when convenient.

"Go ahead, Flore, if that's what you want to do," he said, "but I am not at all comfortable with it…be careful."

Adam came close to putting his foot down and declaring a flat "no", but didn't have the heart to disappoint.

J. R. Dancy's house was delivered September 23rd, a full week ahead of schedule. Adam considered it among his finest work.

After closing at Justin's law office, Dancy took the keys and left without uttering even a compliment for a job well done. Adam was glad to be rid of him. His only regret at this point was agreeing to allow Florecita to help Delores, Dancy's wife, to settle in.

October came, and, now, was almost gone. Florecita had been working three days a week at the Dancy's for a month. She seemed to enjoy getting out of the house, and had become close with Delores.

It was the October, 31st…Halloween. Florecita was always home by four in the afternoon. It was after six and no word from her.

Adam was about to call the Dancy residence when the phone rang.

"Adam, I have been arrested. I am in the city jail."

"What! Why?"

"I have been arrested for something I did not do."

"I'll be right there."

"What's she being held for?" he asked the officer at the front desk.

"Are you her husband?"

"No, she's my fiancée."

"She says she doesn't have any papers," said the man.

"I'm aware of that. Is that why she's here?"

"Not yet, but that'll come."

"Well, why is she here?"

"Attempted theft and assault."

"I don't understand. Please explain."

"Charges were pressed by Mr. J.R. Dancy. It seems your fiancée got caught trying to steal jewelry from the Dancy home. Mrs. Dancy was out when Mr. Dancy came in and surprised her. She proceeded to hit him in the head with a vase…a very expensive one according to Mr. Dancy."

"How much is her bail?"

"I'm afraid there won't be any bail."

"What do you mean? What about her rights."

"She's got no rights here, Mister."

"I need to call my attorney," said Adam.

"OK, but I don't think it'll do any good."

"Why do you say that?"

"She's being turned over to ICE in the morning."

"You mean the immigration people?"

"Yes, Sir, the immigration people."

"Wait a minute…she's pregnant."

"Yes, Sir, I know."

"Can I see her?"

"Yes, Sir, of course. By the way Mr…"

"Clay…Adam Clay."

"J.R. Dancy is a very powerful man in this town. I wouldn't make waves if I were you."

He was led to the back where the jail cells were. They passed a drunk holding his hand out through the bars asking for a cigarette. Two cells down was his Florecita. He stood silently for moment looking through the bars. She was lying on a bunk facing the wall.

"Florecita," he said.

She turned in a jerky motion, jumped up and ran toward him. She clutched the bars that separated them and burst into tears:

"Adam, I did nothing but defend myself."

He put his hands over hers.

"Tell me, Sweetheart…what happened?"

"He came at me. I hit him with a vase. He tried to force himself on me, Adam. Please, believe me. I did nothing wrong.""

"I believe you, my Love, I believe you."

"You were right, Adam. He is an evil man."

As she filled him in on the details of what happened, Adam realized the seriousness of the situation and knew they would need legal help… fast.

"We'll get through this, Florecita. Try to rest, now. I'll be back in the morning."

They kissed through the cold metal bars. He turned, trying to rein in his emotions and walked away.

His parting words to the desk sergeant spewed like a dragon's breath: "That Son-of-a-bitch doesn't know what waves are."

It was after nine p.m. before he was able to get Justin on the phone: "He demanded sex, Justin…after making sure his wife was out-of-pocket. 'Said he was the only thing standing between her being able to be here and getting deported. It didn't seem to matter to the perverted bastard that she was five months pregnant.

"She said he came at her in the kitchen. That's when she broke a vase over his head. After calling 911 and getting the police involved, he insisted on being taken to the hospital in an ambulance. I understand he got six stitches and was sent on his way."

"Were you able to post bail?" asked Justin.

"No, they're turning her over to immigration in the morning. I hear Dancy is using all his political influence to have her sent back to Mexico immediately. They won't even let her come home to get her clothes and personal things.

"I'm sure he intends to get rid of her before his wife gets wind of what's going on. Too many questions could and would come up, especially since Florecita and Mrs. Dancy have become friends."

"It sounds that way," said Justin."

"I know it would be the stupidest thing I ever did, but I have an overwhelming urge to go over to that bastard's house...the one I built for him, and..."

"Yeah," Justin interrupted, "That would be the stupidest thing you ever did."

Chapter 19

There was to be no sleep for Adam Clay this night. He entered the dark empty house that only twenty-four hours before was his and Florecita's home…a place where great affection and hope for the future filled the now empty space. Without her there, it was just a shell…barren and cold. With despair as his only companion, he began gathering a few clothes and personal items she would need until the situation could be resolved. There wasn't much to put in the overnight bag, but everything was special…from the jeans she had on when she first came to clean the house to the toothbrush she faithfully used three times a day.

Later in the evening, as he browsed through pictures taken over the past couple of months, dark clouds of reality began to take shape. His Florecita would not be with him tomorrow. Then came the unthinkable scenario… she may be away from him for the foreseeable future. This could not… would not be.

It seemed as if the night would never end. He tried to escape into sleep, but only an occasional drift into an unsettling half-consciousness was allowed. With restless anticipation he kept looking at his watch. He paced the floor, walked outside, then repeated the routine.

Finally came the first hint of dawn as the eastern sky began to lighten. There was no time to waste. First, he needed to go to the city jail and see if there was a way to head off the deportation procedure. He would not call José, at least not yet. That would only complicate matters in that he himself was undocumented.

Adam made it to the jail at about 6:00 a.m.

"I need to see Flor Valdez," he said to the desk clerk.

"I'm sorry, Sir. They've already come and picked her up."

"Who came and picked her up?"

"ICE, the immigration people."

"Where did they take her?"

"I don't know, to wherever they hold illegals, I guess."

Adam felt his head about to explode: "When did they take her?"

"I'm not sure of the exact time. It was during the night shift. I wasn't here."

It was after ten before Adam was able to find out the location of the ICE holding facility for Montgomery county.

"Do you have a Flore Valdez here? I need to see her."

The woman looked up from her computer screen: "She's not here."

"She's not here? I was told they brought her here from the Montgomery City Jail."

"Well she's not here now. She's on a bus, accompanied by an immigration officer, headed to Mexico.

The mad scramble was on. He had to get to Mexico, find her and bring her back. But, he didn't know where to start, and to make matters worse he didn't have a passport. His head felt heavy…his mind numb. Hardly able to think, he picked up the phone and punched numbers that were hard-wired into his brain.

"*Bueno.*" came from the voice at the other end of the line.

"José, it's me, Adam."

"Adam, are you OK?"

"No, they've deported Florecita, and I've got to get to Mexico…now!"

"Wait, Amigo. Tell me exactly what is going on."

Adam still didn't want to share all the details…at least not yet. He told José someone reported Florecita as being illegal and they took her into custody.

"Where would she go once they get her to Mexico?" Adam asked.

"I'm sure she will try to get to our mother and sister in Mexico City. The immigration officer will only take her as far as the border then put her out. She will be on her own from there. It will be a long and dangerous journey. She will have to travel at least five hundred miles to get there."

"Hell, she's five months pregnant and only thing she has is the cloths on her back. I don't know if she's got any money on her or not. I've got to get there, man, but I don't have a passport. How can I get into Mexico without getting caught?"

"That would be fairly easy," said José, "but you will not know where or how to look for her. You do not know the language well, or how to stay out of trouble. Mexico is much different than here, Adam. I, of course will go, but there may be a better way."

"How…what?"

"Paco."

"Paco! What's he got to do with anything? He's nothing but trouble. I told him to stay away from the family."

"For us, one may leave the family, but the family never leaves them. Paco is still family whether he lives in a different world or not. Listen to what I have to say, Amigo."

"OK, José. I'll listen."

"Paco knows the routes, the people, and how to avoid trouble for himself. He can find her and get her to safety."

"I don't know how to get in touch with him, José."

"I do," José replied.

"I will start trying to contact Paco immediately, and instruct him to go the fastest way possible to El Paso and to the border crossing at Juárez where Florecita will be put out. From there he will escort her to Mexico City, and deliver her safely to our mother's place."

"What if he can't or won't do it?" said Adam.

"He will do it, Adam…trust me."

Adam agreed to José's plan. Though made in haste, it seemed workable.

Within an hour of his discussion with José, Adam was applying for a passport.

"How long will it take?" he asked the postal clerk handling his application.

"Six to eight weeks," came the reply as the photo was being taken.

"I don't have that long."

"Well, you can fast-track it for an extra sixty bucks…still no guarantees."

"Fast-track it," said Adam.

"I should be able to cash out at around $150,000," said Adam during the afternoon meeting at Justin's office. "Then, there's the $200,000 in mutual funds that my father left me. I want you to have Power-of-Attorney and be in control of everything. After I leave, I want you to sell everything…the house, stocks, the vehicles, the tools and equipment…everything. I'll set up an account in Mexico where you can transfer funds to."

"Are you sure that's what you want to do?" said Justin, "You'll be burning all the bridges you've worked so hard to build."

"Yes, I want to burn them all. I'm done with this place."

"What's your plan once you get to Mexico, Adam?"

"I don't have an immediate one. Maybe I'll be the 'illegal' for a change…in Mexico."

"That doesn't sound too practical."

"It certainly isn't practical to bring her back here. Look, Justin, all I know at this point is that I am going to be with Florecita. I'll be out of here as soon as my passport comes, and I don't know when…or if I'll be back."

Adam's cell phone rang during the conversation:

"Hello."

"Paco is on his way," said the voice at the other end. It was José.

"Good, how is he getting there?"

"Luck is with us, Amigo. He was already in Texas when I tracked him down, not far from El Paso. He said he will take care of everything."

"Thank you, José. Keep me posted, OK."

"OK, Adam…*adios*."

"Thank God," said Adam after the call, "Paco's going to pick Florecita up at the border and take her to Mexico City where her mother and sister live."

"I thought Paco went bad and is now involved with one of the drug cartels," said Justin.

"I don't care if he's the devil's son…or who he's involved with as long as he gets her to safety."

Adam abruptly changed the subject: "I'm going to make José foreman if he will take the job. I need somebody I can rely on to tie up loose ends after I'm gone, and until it is time for you to shut the company down for me. He will be signing company checks as needed, and reporting everything to you."

"Isn't that risky allowing him to have access to the company account?"

"It's the least risky thing I'm doing, Justin. I'd trust this man with my life."

"You are taking a leap of faith, aren't you?"

"Yes, I am, aren't I?"

Three days passed without hearing from Paco. His heart raced every time the phone rang, thinking that perhaps it was news of the whereabouts of his Florecita.

"Why the hell aren't we hearing from Paco?" snapped Adam.

"Be patient, *Amigo*. Sometimes it is difficult to communicate by cell phone in Mexico."

Along with his desperate concern for Florecita's well-being and getting to Mexico, there was a lingering gnaw in the mind of Adam Clay…Dancy. With great difficulty Adam held steady.

The call came the fourth day after her departure:

"Adam, it is me."

"Florecita!" he shouted, "Where are you?"

"In Mexico City. Paco found me as I was being put out at the border. He brought me here to my mother's place."

"Are you OK? How do you feel?"

"I am OK, but very tired."

"How did you 'all get from the border to Mexico City?"

"We came by bus. It was a long hard journey…I am so tired. Can you come for me, Adam?"

"Yes, *mi Amor*, as soon as I receive my passport. I'll be there soon…I promise. How can I stay in touch with you in the meantime?"

"We have no phone here at my mother's place. I am on Paco's cell phone, but we had to climb a hill behind her casa to get reception. I am so tired," she repeated, her voice fading.

"You go and rest, now, sweetheart. Let me speak to Paco."

"This is Paco," said the voice at the other end.

"Paco, it's Adam. Before anything else is said, I want to thank you. I don't know how I can ever repay you for what you've done."

"No need to repay, Amigo, just give me a little understanding."

"I'll do my best, mi Amigo."

Paco's voice began to break up, then suddenly there was static and reception was completely lost. Though disappointed that he wasn't able to talk more with her, at least he knew that she was safe. A huge burden was lifted. Now, the only thing standing between him and his Floricita was a passport, or the lack thereof.

November slipped into December. With the holiday spirit taking hold, decorations went up, crowds of shoppers took to the streets, and scores of festive activities began. For Adam, there was no Christmas spirit or thought of celebration…only the anxiety of not being with her.

"Why is it taking so freakin' long to get a simple passport?" he ranted to Justin. "If I ran my business like the government runs theirs, I'd be out of business within a month."

Then, came Christmas Eve. He wondered about his Florecita…how she was feeling… what she and her family would be doing on this holy night. He had never felt so lonely, but without her, there was nothing or no one that could offer comfort.

For the first time in years he decided to pray…not to ask for anything, but just for a little company.

It was a little after dark when he went to his mailbox. A single letter lay there. The first thing he noticed once back inside was that there was no return address, but immediately he recognized the handwriting. The post mark stamp read Nov. 6, 2011. He tore into it and read:

Mi Amor,
I just arrive. The trip was hard, and I no feel well.
I hurt for you so bad. I miss your face and your touch.
I miss your voice that comfort me so.
Please come for me as soon as possible.
Te Amo,
Flor

He spent the evening reading over and over the five broken sentences…and losing himself in thought.

At least I have a little part of her here with me tonight.

A week later the new year '2012' arrived, yielding neither a passport or reprieve from the anxiety he suffered .

It came January 11th. Finally, after almost two and a half months of waiting, he held the passport in his hands.

Immediately, he was on the phone with American Airlines. There was no time to waste. Florecita was now in her eighth month. He booked his flight. At last, everything was on go. Ticketed and packed, he was scheduled to depart on the eve of Friday the 13th. He declared this Friday the 13th his lucky day…for others, maybe not.

There would be a six hour layover in Dallas because of his rush in booking, but that was ok. He was just grateful for being able to get a flight this soon. Now, all he needed was to go over some final details with José and get instructions on how to get to Florecita's mother's place. They met at José's apartment that afternoon.

"My flight is scheduled for 9:00 tomorrow evening, said Adam. I'll leave my jeep in the airport parking lot with the ticket and keys in the glove compartment. Can you pick it up when you get a chance and take it to my house? You know where I keep the key."

"Sí, I will take care of it, Adam."

"Thank you for acting as foreman for my company. It will be shut down as soon as all the warranty work is done. Keep in close touch with Justin Walker."

"Yes, of course," said José.

"Now, how do I get to your mother's house once I arrive in Mexico City?"

José took a sheet of paper, wrote a paragraph in Spanish and handed it to Adam.

"Give this to the taxi driver," he said.

"Is there anything else I should know or be aware of?" asked Adam.

"It is in a very poor section of the city," said José. "Good people live there, but still, it is dangerous. Just be cautious."

"How much trouble will I have with language?"

"You should be able to get by. Many now speak English. Our little sister, Maria, speaks it some…and by the way, your Spanish is better than you think, mi *Amigo*. You've learned a lot since we met back in March."

"Thanks, that gives me a little more confidence. I'll call and give you an update as soon as possible," said Adam.

"*Bueno*," José replied.

"Well, I best be going now. Take care my friend."

There was a brief pause as the two men stood eye to eye. Both knew there was nothing more to say. They shook hands, then hugged in traditional Hispanic fashion.

"Good luck, Adam. Take with you my love for my mother and sisters."

Chapter 20

As darkness fell on the evening of departure, Adam intended to take care of some unfinished business on his way to the airport. Something he had told no one about, held inside…something that had nagged and become an overwhelming obsession. He punched the numbers in on his cell phone.

"J.R. Dancy speaking."

"J.R. this Adam Clay."

"Yes," said the obviously surprised voice responding in a formal manner and tone, "What can I do for you, Mr. Clay."

"I just got word that a hazardous device was mistakenly installed on the electrical system of your house. It will cause a fire. I need to come by immediately and take it off."

"Can't this wait until tomorrow? My family and I are fixing to sit down for dinner."

"No. Your house can go up in flames at any time. It won't take but a few minutes to correct the situation. I'm in front of your house now; so I won't knock."

The door opened allowing a pleasant aroma of home cooking to escape into the brisk evening air.

"Well, come on in and do what you've got to do," said Dancy without making eye contact.

"We need to go to your home-office. That's where I will start dismantling things."

Having built the house, Adam knew every square inch of it.

Dancy's study was a man-space to be envied. Among the luxuries boasted in this twenty foot by twenty foot room were cherry wood wainscot panels, coffered ceilings and a wall of bookshelves.

When they entered, Dancy went immediately to the large ornate desk located in the middle of the room and stood behind it.

Adam closed the door and walked to the front of the desk. He was face to face with Dancy.

"You know why I'm here, don't you J.R."

"I assume to fix something that will catch my house on fire."

"Your house is already on fire, Mister."

"What do you mean by that?"

"Oh…you don't know? Well then, what did you mean by using all of your influence to have Flore Valdez deported. She was to be my wife…but you knew that. What did you mean by setting my house on fire?"

"Flore Valdez tried to steal from me…and assaulted me."

"That's not exactly the way I heard it."

"I think it's time for you to go, Mr. Clay," said Dancy, his finger in dial position on the lit pad of his cell phone.

"No, Mother Fucker, I think it may be time for you to go."

"Adam reached in his pocket and pulled out the old 38 service revolver, a leftover from World War II given to him by his grandfather.

With his right arm straight out he pointed it directly at Dancy's head:

"Ready to go, J.R?"

"What the hell are you doing Clay? Don't you know the consequences of this?"

"I know exactly what I'm doing."

Then, waving his hands in front of him as if shooing away flies, Dancy cried out:

"No! Wait! Don't do it! I'll get her back! I'll do whatever you want! For God's sake don't do it."

"Is that the phone you used to call the police on Flor Valdez?"

There was no reply.

"Give it to me," said Adam, the gun still aimed at Dancy's head.

Trembling, Dancy reached out over the desk to hand over the phone. Adam grabbed his arm and dragged him across the desktop. The phone flew from his hand. Pens, papers and Dancy's name plaque tumbled from the desk.

As he lay there flat on his stomach, Adam's left hand came down and grasped the back of his neck. Dancy's head lay left side down pressed against the unforgiving desktop surface. Adam jammed the gun hard into Dancy's right cheek, twisting the barrel back and forth in a taunting fashion.

"There's six chambers in this thing," said Adam.

Without another word, he let go of Dancy's neck long enough to give the chamber a spin.

"I have no idea what the next click will bring. Either way, J.R., this is where your hell begins."

He pulled back the hammer until it clicked.

"No!" pleaded Dancy.

Adam squeezed the trigger.

"CLICK"

He shoved Dancy backward across the desk, causing him to land slouched in his plush executive office chair.

Holding his heart, Dancy slumped and looked up at Adam. His eyes said it all.

Adam stomped on the phone several times.

"Trust me, J.R., this is just the beginning. Now, go and enjoy supper with your family…I have to go back to my hell."

"By the way, here's something to think about before calling the cops regarding our little prayer meeting this evening. Just visualize tomorrow's news: 'Claims have been made that on Halloween night of last year J. Roland Dancy, prominent attorney and political heavyweight attempted to rape an undocumented alien that he had illegally working in his home while his wife was out with their kids trick or treating. It's alleged that he used his influence to have Flor Valdez immediately deported.'

"I'll bet Mrs. Dancy will be impressed."

Adam slipped the gun back into his pocket.

"Don't bother to get up," he said, "I'll show myself out."

Delores Dancy was setting the dining room table as Adam made his way towards the foyer.

"Did you fix the problem, Mr. Clay?" she asked.

"I think so. I'll be checking back. Have a good evening, Mrs. Dancy."

He made his exit.

Even though he felt that Dancy, under threat of exposure, would not call the police, Adam wanted to take no further chances. He wasted no time hightailing it towards the airport. Along the way he stopped and threw the gun and bullets in a gutter drain pipe. There were no bullets in the chamber. He removed them just before going into Dancy's house, deciding that if he did shoot the S.O.B., his mission could, and most likely would, be compromised.

He arrived at the airport with perfect timing, just as planned.

Chapter 21

Adam looked out the window of the slowly descending jet. As the engines throttled back and wispy clouds passed, big treeless rust-colored mountains came into view. To him, the barren landscape appeared to be composed of iron-ore and red clay. It was far from the green of Alabama.

In the great level valley beneath the mountains lay a patchwork of roads and structures giving evidence of a heavily populated area.

"This is the captain speaking. We are now making our final approach to Mexico City International Airport. I hope you have had a pleasant experience flying American Airlines. We will be landing in approximately six minutes. Please fasten your seatbelts."

Adam leaned back in his seat and looked out the window as the ground got closer. Then came a thud as the wheels made contact with the runway.

He looked at his watch…8:04 a.m.

For whatever reason, Mexico City was in the central time zone…the same as Montgomery. From what he could tell so far, that was about the only thing the two cities had in common.

Mexico City International Airport could swallow up Montgomery International Airport at least twenty times. People were everywhere. The crowd was of varied ethnic makeup…much more than that of South Alabama where most commuters were either Anglo or African American. He did note that, here, there were very few blacks in the mix.

After retrieving his two suitcases from the luggage conveyor he stepped outside. The first thing noticeable was the smell…a mixture of sulfur, sewer gas odors and exhaust fumes. An early morning haze hung over the city giving evidence of a serious pollution problem. And, the air was different…thinner. He was aware that Mexico was almost a mile and a half above sea level whereas Montgomery was less than three- hundred feet.

Feeling light-headed, his body needed some time to adjust to this new environment.

Another noticeable difference was temperature…from a chilly forty degrees Fahrenheit at departure in Alabama to a milder sixty degree January morning in Mexico City. This gave him a better understanding as to why, for the most part, there were no heating or cooling systems here as Florecita had explained.

After briefly assessing his surroundings he hailed a cab:

"Do you speak English?" he asked the driver.

"*Sí, Señor*," came the reply, "My name is Moises. Just call me Moses. That will be easier for you to remember."

The middle aged Mexicano's thin mustache turned up as he grinned: "Here is my card, Señor. If you should need any other services, I can provide anything from a Rolex watch to a woman."

Adam took the card and slipped it into his shirt pocket:

"I need to go here," said Adam as he handed over the folded piece of paper with directions on it written by José.

Moses unfolded it and rubbed his chin: "I will have to charge you extra," he said, "We will be going through some bad areas."

It's already started, thought Adam: *'the fleecing of the Gringo.'*

"OK, let's go," he said

Never had Adam seen anything like the traffic in this town. Cars, taxis, buses and motorcycles jammed the streets. There was a constant honking of horns, much hand shaking from windows of frustrated drivers, and obscenities blaring from within one vehicle or another.

Cars would get within inches of each other, but somehow avoided collision. It was reminiscent of a flock of birds that could instinctively change directions on a dime without flying into each other. Evidently, thought Adam, drivers in Mexico City have the same instinct. He decided to relax and leave the driving to Moses.

"What brings you to Mexico, *Señor*?" asked Moses.

"My fiancée is here. She had to leave the states…no papers."

"You speak a little differently than most Americanos. What part are you from?"

"Alabama," Adam replied.

"Ahh, I heard Alabama was cracking down on those without papers. I have kin that resides there. They live in constant fear of being deported."

"Well, they have good reason to be afraid. Believe me, I know."

The morning haze was lifting, and it looked as if it would be a clear day after all. The smells had somewhat dissipated. ..either that or he had gotten used to them. And, he felt himself acclimating to the thinner air.

They began driving through some rough looking areas with a lot of loitering and craggy looking characters on the streets. They all stared with what appeared to be more than curiosity as the cab passed.

"My cousin, Guillermo, was kidnapped here last month," said Moses, "He also drives a cab. It cost my family six hundred pesos to free him. That is almost fifty US dollars."

They drove on for another few miles.

"We are arriving," announced Moses.

Adam looked at his watch. It was almost ten o'clock as they entered the hamlet called *Tierra de Lola*, or as translated, Lola Land. The village existed on the northeastern outskirts of the mighty metropolitan city of Mexico DF. As expected, the area was rundown. But, even after being warned Adam was surprised at what he saw. All of its buildings, without exception, had by any standard long outlived their usefulness…but still, all were in use for one purpose or another…sometimes as habitat for squatters. The streets were narrow and in poor condition. Cinder block dwellings scattered about, some jammed up to each other and were little more than tin roofed shacks. Jury-rigged wires ran all over the place in what looked like feeble attempts to get electricity to the dwellings. Clothes lines dominated what little there was of green spaces.

Even with all its third worldness, this place held some oddball charm in the eyes of Adam Clay. Maybe it was because he knew his Florecita was here, and he was just minutes from being with her.

"This is it, *Señor*," said Moses, pointing to the approximate twenty foot wide block structure that lay ten or so yards ahead, squeezed in among a crowded mix of shanties. Adam paid the fair and exited the cab: "Thanks for bringing me here," he said, with a better understanding of why he had to pay extra.

"Good luck, *Amigo*," said Moses. "Remember to call me if you need something." He then backed up, turned around, and drove away.

Adam's heart raced as he made his way towards the dwelling. Then, there he was, standing just outside. The door was open. He stood at the entry a moment and stared into the dark little room.

"Hello...*hola*...anyone at home?"

There was silence.

In the far corner was a bed with someone in it balled up under the covers.

"I'm Adam Clay, looking for Florecita Valdez."

Just then the figure in the bed threw the covers back and turned towards him.

"Adam, *mi Amor*, I thought you would never be here. I thought I might never see you again. Come...come," she said.

He rushed to her, and held her close. She clung to him.

"Nothing could keep me away from you, Flore...nothing or no one."

Releasing all the pent-up feelings he kissed her, caressed her face, then held her even more close.

She responded likewise, but after a few minutes he knew something was not as it should be: "How do you feel?" he asked.

"I'm so sorry Adam, but I do not feel very well. I stay weak and sometimes suffer pain. My mother and sister do the best they can, but I sometimes feel I cannot make it."

"Have you seen a doctor since you've been here?"

"No, but I am in the care of a midwife. She says there is no sign of danger...that my problem is most likely in my head...missing you."

"We need to get you out of here...to someplace where proper care can be given."

"Not right now, *mi* Amor. I am sure I will be better now that you are here."

Just then, a dim light came on from the ceiling, and a female voice interrupted.

"*Florecita, keen esta aquí?*"

Adam looked towards the entry. There, stood the shadowy figure of a woman.

"*Este es Adam Ma,ma.*"

The woman came forward. Adam stood as she came face to face with him. The slightly stooped gray-haired lady was the same he had seen in a photo at Jose's place the year before.

Her dark eyes looked into Adam's much as Florecita did. She reached out, took his hand, then raised on her toes and kissed him on the cheek: "*Bienvenido, Senor* Adam…*gracious por venir.*"

"Tell your mother that I will be here for you and her…and the baby when it comes."

Florecita relayed the message. Margarita's eyes welled as she smiled.

Adam looked at her, smiled and nodded as an acknowledging gesture. He then looked around the room. A dull whitewash covered the walls. Just to the right of a door to a back room was a sink and countertop. On top of the countertop set a hotplate. Above, hung a plastic figurine of Jesus on the cross along with a picture of the Madonna. Next to the countertop was a rusting refrigerator and wood burning stove. A small window was in the middle of the cinder block wall to the right. On that wall was a corkboard with photos of family members pinned to it. He immediately recognized José, Juan and Paco. Besides these things, and the bed where Florecita lay, there was a table some chairs and not much more. The floor was a rough concrete slab with worn area rugs spread about.

"Do you have a bathroom?" he asked.

"*Si, el baño* is in the next room," said Florecita.

"May I?" he said.

"Of course, and we will find you a bed to be next to me."

Adam walked into the next room. There were two single beds, a chair, a chest-of-drawers, a small dressing table with a clouded de-silvering mirror attached, and nothing more. At the other end of the room in an enclosed area was a cramped bathroom with toilet, sink and shower. Next to it was a closet with no door. A curtain covered the opening.

As his eyes adjusted to his darkened surroundings, he noted that in spite of its primitiveness, the place was spotlessly clean.

He smiled as he entered the tiny bathroom thinking that the cleanliness gene must run in this family. He relieved himself, then rejoined Florecita and her mother.

It wasn't long before another figure entered the dimly lit room.

"This is my sister, Maria," said Florecita, "She can speak a little English."

Even without makeup or pampered grooming, Maria, like her sister, was striking.

"*Hola*, Maria. I'm Adam. I guess you know who I am."

"Sí, Señor, I know well who you are."

Chapter 22

T he first thing that needed to be done was to make room for Adam in the small dwelling. He had traveled light. Two suitcases held every-thing …all he would possess for the foreseeable future. He did have cash… enough to last awhile. Thirty neatly folded one hundred dollar bills lay hidden in the money belt he ordered on line shortly after Florecita's depor-tation. In addition, he carried a thousand dollars in twenties and fifties on his person…two hundred at all times in his wallet…the rest in his shoes.

"I know to where we can get a bed," said Maria in broken English.

Adam accompanied her up the half-paved pothole ridden street. They passed some young boys kicking a soccer ball about. A woman hung clothes on a line stretched between two shacks. Several men, some young some old, looked on curiously at young Maria and her gringo companion.

They walked the distance of about two city blocks through the little jungle of shanties until they came upon a structure much larger than the rest. Its exterior was stucco instead of bare cinder block and was obviously well-maintained.

"This is the home of Pedro. He owns many of the houses here including the place where we live. We pay to him rent each month. I am sure he will have a bed and other things we may need. You can talk with him. He speaks much better English than me."

She called out in front of the open door: "*Señor Pedro.*"

After a minute or so, a dark porky mustached man of about forty came to the entry.

"*Hola, Maria. Que pasa.*"

"*Este es Señor Adam. El es esposo de mi hermana,* Florecita. Speak in English, *por favor.*"

The two men shook hands: "What can I do for you, *Señor Adam.*"

"I will be staying with Maria and her family for a while. I need to purchase a bed. Anything will do."

"I have a cot I can sell to you for," he paused and rubbed his chin, "for ten US dollars."

"I'll tell you what, Señor Pedro," said Adam, "if you can include a pillow and two blankets I can pay twenty US dollars."

"*Sí, Señor*, I can do that. I will return in a few moments."

"Pedro went into his house and as he said he would returned in a few moments with an army cot, two blankets and a pillow.

Adam pulled out his wallet, took out a twenty, handed it to Pedro, then hoisted the cot over his shoulders.

"Wait," said Pedro, "I have a push wagon out back. You can use it."

"Thank you," said Adam, "I'll return it as soon as we get things unloaded."

Adam knew that he would probably need outside help before things were over. He intended to establish and maintain a good relationship with Pedro, the community kingpin.

Florecita's condition didn't seem to be improving. She could get out of bed for short periods of time, but there was always chronic fatigue and general discomfort. She was in the third trimester, over eight months along. Every time Adam started insisting on getting her to a doctor, she replied: "Let's wait a little longer, *mi Amor*. I think I'm getting better."

"We're not waiting any longer, Florecita. We're either getting a doctor out here to check you out or we're going into town."

"There are no doctors here, Adam…only 'Curers.' They are who we use to treat illnesses."

"I'm not having any of this home grown doctoring, Flor. I want a qualified physician to examine you."

He pulled Moses's, the taxi driver's card out of his wallet, and punched in the number on his cell phone. There was no signal…no connection. He went outside and moved around to several spots…still no signal. Remembering Florecita had called on Paco's phone from a hill behind her mother's house, he headed there. On its level knoll was a large cypress tree. Scattered about were wooden crosses and flat rocks with names and dates either painted or carved on them. He punched in the numbers and got a connection.

"Moses, this is Adam Clay, the guy you brought to Lola Land two days ago…remember me?"

"*Sí, Señor*, I remember."

"Look, I need to get a doctor out here…a good one. My fiancée is eight and a half months pregnant and having problems. I want the best Doc. I can get…one familiar with pregnancies. Can you help?"

"Sí, Señor, I know exactly who to bring, but it will probably be tomorrow before he will be able to come."

"That's OK, just bring him…and thank you, Moses."

Around noon the next day Moses arrived with an older, kindly looking man with a full snow-white beard. Moses introduced him.

"*Señor* Adam, this is Dr. Gonzales. He cared for my wife and delivered my children. This is how I know he is the best."

"Pleased to meet you, sir," said Adam.

The elder man nodded: "The pleasure is mine, *Señor*."

"Dr. Gonzales is retired," said Moses, "and now does charity work."

"Thank you for coming," said Adam.

Gonzales nodded as he entered the dimly lit room. Moses waited outside. The family looked on as he opened his black bag, first taking out a stethoscope. During the examination he asked Florecita a lot of questions…in Spanish. She calmly answered each one. Adam began feeling confident that Moses had brought the right man to look after his Florecita.

After fifteen or so minutes he turned to Adam:

"She is anemic and dehydrated. I also see signs of extreme exhaustion. Has she been under any unusual stress during the pregnancy?"

"Yes," said Adam, "She had a rough journey from the states to here."

"I am going to give her a shot that should improve her level of energy. You know it as vitamin B-12. And, I am leaving some iron tablets for her to take daily. She must take a lot of fluids and stay confined to bed."

"Do you think I should get her out of here…take her into town close to a hospital?" Adam asked.

"No, I would not advise moving her at this time. Keep her in bed. I will come next week to see how she is doing."

Florecita began feeling somewhat better the next day. For the most part Margarita had been caring for and keeping her company. Besides what seemed to be endless conversation between the two, in Spanish of course, they spent much of their time knitting…Margarita making a blue infant's sweater, Florecita making a pink one.

"Don't you and your mother ever run out of something to talk about?" he asked.

"*No, Mi Amore*…never."

"Well, what do you all talk about?"

"The family, the sorrows, Jesus…you….and,,,"

"OK, I get it."

There was little verbal communication between Adam and Margarita. Yet, they seemed to do fine with hand gestures, a little of his broken Spanish, a little of her broken English, and sometimes exaggerated facial expressions. He took notice that at one time she must have been a beauty much the same as her daughters were. Her classic features, however, had for the most part given way to the weathering lines of age and a hard life. Yet, those dark eyes shown through…sparkling at times like a young girl. She was a humble woman who in silent words expressed appreciation for him being there. Adam found himself growing more and more attached to her…and obviously her to him. He felt as if they were all truly becoming a family… something he had never really known. He started calling her, "Mamacita."

Adam decided to start making some long overdue repairs to the dwelling, as in repairing roof leaks, plumbing leaks and shoring up the jacklegged electrical conglomeration. To him it was a miracle that the place hadn't caught fire a long time ago.

Sometimes, he accompanied Maria to the little market a half-mile away where she worked. They would ride her raggedy Vespa motor scooter, the only transportation the family had. He would buy groceries, sometimes pick up something at the adjoining hardware store, ride back home with the groceries, ride back to the market, leave the scooter for Maria to return home after work, then himself walk back home. He was well aware that it was a most inefficient way to conduct things, but what would never work in the fast pace of his past life worked well here in the little shanty town of Lola Land.

As Adam walked home from the market, he always felt the watching eyes. It didn't make him feel threatened, though. What else should he expect…a stranger, especially a gringo on turf where he was not familiar? He passed it all off as normal curiosity.

Adam noticed some potted flowers, daisies, at the hardware store. *el Señor* Moreno, the store owner, said it was unheard of for daisies to bloom in January. Yet, there they were, in full bloom. He bought all six and with great care planted them in front of the little dwelling. Not that it was much of an aesthetic improvement, a greater purpose was served. Florecita and her mother were thrilled.

"You are so thoughtful, Adam my love. Did you know that my mother's name, 'Margarita' means 'daisy' in Spanish?"

"I had no idea."

"You have made her feel very special…and me too."

In the evening, after supper, usually of rice or beans, tortillas, chicken or sometimes pork, and, after Margarita and Maria had retired to their beds in the next room, he would lie beside Florecita on the old worn army cot. They would talk.

"Do you love me?" she asked this particular evening.

"Yes, I love you. You know that."

"I want us to be together forever, Adam."

"I want the same, sweetheart, and we will be."

"Will you love me always?"

"Yes, I will always love you."

"If I die, will you take care of our baby?"

"Don't talk like that, Flor. I would never let you leave me."

"Will you marry me…tomorrow?"

"Yes, I would marry you tonight if I could."

"Tomorrow, by a priest…can we?"

Chapter 23

Morning came. A shaft of light showed through the room's only window, relieving somewhat the darkness. He looked over at Florecita. She was sleeping peacefully. During the night, his thoughts focused on fulfilling her wish.

Maria came from the back room: "Where can I find a priest?" he asked.

"There is a Father Lopez who comes here sometimes as a social worker. His Parrish is about three kilometers from here."

"Can you go with me there, Maria?"

"*Sí*, may I ask for what reason?"

"I'm going to marry your sister…today."

Her eyes lit up followed by a broad smile.

"We can go now if you wish."

They set out on the Vespa. Maria steered. Adam sat behind her. As always, he felt the watching eyes following them along the route.

The two arrived at the little church at about 10:00 a.m.

Father Lopez was a clean-cut pleasant looking man somewhere in his thirties.

"Father Lopez, this is *Señor* Adam Clay," said Maria, "He needs to speak with you."

"How can I help you *Señor*," asked the Priest?"

"Father," Adam begun, "My fiancée lies in bed not far from here. She is eight and a half months pregnant and having difficulties. I made a promise to her…that I would do everything in my power for us to be married today. Will you help us?"

"What you ask is impossible Señor. There is paperwork, procedures and counseling before I can perform a marriage ceremony."

"Father, if you can only say the words…let us take the vow, and do the paperwork and procedures later."

"I'm sorry Señor, but…"

"Look," interrupted Adam, "I will give you five-hundred US dollars that you can use to do good work in your parish. Now, don't you think God will allow you to make an exception to the rules this time? I don't care if you never file the papers. I just want the words, the vows and the blessing."

"The priest took pause. He looked up and silently gazed toward the sky as if counseling with the almighty himself. In a few moments he crossed himself, lowered his head and looked straight into Adam's eyes:

"When do you want this to take place, Señor?"

"Now," Adam replied.

At her bedside, Florecita and Adam took the sacred vows that would bind them to one another for the rest of their lives. Lopez delivered the words in Spanish, then slowly repeated them in English. Tears streamed down the face of both Maria and Margarita as they stood witness in the small room lit only by a single bulb in the ceiling and what light was afforded by the window and open door.

"I don't even have a ring to offer you," said Adam

"I do not need one," she replied. "You are my ring, *mí Amore.*"

Just then, Margarita took the wedding band from her finger and handed it to Adam.

"Enrique, her father would have wanted her to have it," she said.

Adam placed it on his bride's finger. "Thank you," he said.

Father Lopez stayed for supper. There was the usual menu of beans, rice, tortillas and chicken served with spicy mole gravy. A pitcher of rice water sat in the middle of the small table.

As would be expected, dinner conversation was in Spanish. Adam understood some of what was being said, but when need be Florecita translated.

It seemed that Leonardo Lopez's life was a story within itself. He was one among the thousands of Mexico City's street kids. These were abandoned children who survived on the city streets only by their wit and tenacity. There was little hope of escape from this life, however, Leonardo was rescued by a kindly priest who found him lying in an alley, beaten and abused. The priest introduced the youngster to a world of compassion and brotherhood. As Leonardo put it, "A light came over me that changed everything. I was reborn into a world where I serve only God."

It had been three weeks since Adam's arrival when late in the mid-February night Florecita called out:

"*mi Amor*, I think it is time."

If so, this would be several weeks earlier than expected.

He looked at his watch: 11:55.

"What are you feeling, Flore?" he asked.

"The pain is sharp…like a knife." She winced.

After a few moments the pain subsided.

Then, shortly afterward, she cried out: "Adam, the pain is great." Her face and brow broke out in a sweat. He held her hand, "squeeze," he said, "squeeze harder."

Then, again, there was a reprieve. She settled down for the moment and went into a state of calm. He took the opportunity to enter the next room:

"Maria, Flor is in labor. You and your mother need to come."

Maria shook her mother. "*Ven*, Mamá," she shouted. The two came immediately and began trying to give comfort to Florecita.

Adam looked at Maria who was patting her forehead with a damp rag:

"You said there is a midwife who has already seen your sister."

"Sí," she replied.

"Does she live close to here?"

"Not too far?"

"Quickly, go get her."

Maria left immediately, leaving Adam and Margarita there to do what they could.

Adam put the cell phone to his ear and pointed to it: "I will call Doctor Gonzales," he said.

Margarita nodded: "*Sí.*"

He grabbed his flashlight and rushed out the door just as Florecita was having another contraction. He heard her screams as he raced towards *'La Colina de la Muerte,'* the "Hill of the Dead," as it was called by the locals…the only place in the area where his phone would connect to the outside world. He intended to reach Moses and get Dr. Gonzales out there, even though it was well after midnight.

He reached the top. A mist hung close to the ground. There was an eerie silence.

"Damn," no signal, "Try again," no signal, no signal, no signal.

"You son of a bitch," he shouted, "You worked the other day. Why don't you work now?"

He looked at his watch: 12:50. Almost an hour had passed since Florecita's contractions had begun.

He tried again…still no signal. Then, it flashed in his mind, Dr. Gonzales is supposed to come today. Maybe she can hold off until then.

He rushed back down the hill and to the *casa*. Maria was there but, no midwife.

"Where is the midwife?"

"She is away visiting a cousin in another state."

Forecita's contractions were getting closer together.

We'll have to do this ourselves," he said. "Maria get between her legs and be ready to take the baby when it comes. Tell your mother to heat some water and get a blanket or something to wrap the baby in."

In the next moment, Margarita blurted something in Spanish…staccato and as rapid as machine gun fire. Her tone was that of a drill sergeant barking orders.

"Mamá says that she knows exactly what to do…that she has done this before."

Adam decided that he best served by trying to give comfort and encouragement to Florecita. He sat by her side, held her hands and softly repeated the words he knew well in Spanish: "*Tu eres mi amor, Te amo mi corizon…* I love you my Flor. It will be over soon."

A pre-dawn chill filled the room.

Florecita writhed on the bed crying out for Adam in between moans. Margarita took Maria's position so as to receive the baby herself.

"*Puja*," she shouted, "*Puja.*"

Florecita's eyes shut until they became only slits below her brow, and her lips tightened as she strained and tried to push.

Finally, with one last heave, it happened. Margarita pulled and Florecita gave a sigh. It was over.

"*Es una niña*" proclaimed Maria, "a girl."

Chapter 24

Adam looked at his watch: almost 6:30 in the morning. A slap on the behind by Margarita jump-started the new arrival.

The clear cry signaled that the newborn was breathing on her own and everything was normal.

Margarita cut and tied the umbilical cord as Maria held the baby. Adam continued holding Florecita's hand. He was seeing a side of his '*Mamacita*' that he had not seen before…a woman who knew how to take charge in a crisis.

"We have a daughter, My Love," he said to Florecita in a whisper.

She turned to him with her eyes half-closed, and smiled, but said nothing.

Then, Maria brought her the baby wrapped in a small blanket made from cuts of spare cloth.

Her eyes opened more, her smile widened, and a tear rolled down her cheek.

"I would like to call her Lupe, for she is our little miracle. Do you mind, Adam?"

"Of course not," he said. "That's a wonderful name for her."

She held the baby to her breast and began to nurse. He saw a content-ment in her that he had never seen before. She looked up at him and smiled:

"You have made my life complete, *Señor*. I am very grateful…" then, "Adam, I feel so weak. I cannot hold her anymore."

He took the babe and held her in his arms. There she was…so tiny, in-nocent, so perfect. He felt his life complete, too.

"*Mamá*," Maria cried out, "*Ella sigue sangrando* – she still bleeds."

Margarita rushed to her and began inserting rags in a feeble attempt to stop the bleeding.

"I feel myself fading, *mi Amor*," said Florecita as he felt her grip on his hand loosen.

"Take the ring from my finger. Save it for Maria."

"No," he said, "we'll be together forever."

"Take care of Lupe, *mí Amore*. Take care of yourself…and the family…I think I must sleep now."

He watched as her eyes closed and her head slowly turned to the side.

"She's asleep," he said.

"No!" cried Margarita as she ran to her daughter, grabbed her shoulders and began to shake.

"*"Regressa, Flor, Regressa!*" (Come back, Come back!)

There was no response. She then started slapping her face.

"Despertarse, despertarse! – wake up, wake up!" she commanded.

"Stop, Margarita, *alto!"* he shouted.

Suddenly, the world was in slow motion. His brain was numb…barely processing. He watched Margarita drape herself over his Florecita…wailing, sobbing, repeatedly crying out, *"No, No, No!"*

He looked over at Maria… her hand clasped over her mouth… her expression…stunned disbelief…her eyes…wet…tears streaking down her cheeks. He looked on the wall at the statuette of Jesus on the cross…the picture of Mother Mary next to him. He looked down at the babe in his arms. He was lost in some confused state of being, his senses dulled to the point that he was having great difficulty understanding anything.

"No puede ser! - This cannot be," cried Maria.

But, this was…reality at its rawest. His Florecita was gone…that quick…peacefully, but that quick.

As he desperately tried to get the world back in focus, the baby started crying. Immediately, Margarita rose from her daughter and in an urgent tone said something to Maria.

"We must give nourishment to the baby," she translated, "Mamā is going to try to get her to nurse from Flor before it is too late."

With that said, Adam handed the babe to Margarita and went outside into the gloomy overcast morning air. He raised his arms above his head. With elbows bent and hands spread wide, it was as if he was trying to lift the dark curtain that just befell him and the family. He felt pressure in every cell of his body, especially his face. It was as if his face was about to explode, but no tears would come to relieve the pressure.

The spell was broken by Maria:

"Adam," she said with tears streaming, "I...," she hesitated.

He held out his arms: "Come," he said.

She ran to him and clung like a child. With her arms around his waist and her head on his chest, he stroked her hair: "I will always be here for you and your mother, Maria."

Then, he looked deep into her dark eyes. For a moment, he was looking into those of Florecita.

Suddenly...simultaneously, they broke...sobbing, holding one another as all that was pent up surfaced.

It wasn't long before Margarita came out with Lupe in her arms. She spoke to Maria, and again what she said was translated for Adam.

"We have a relative not far from here who herself has a newborn," she relayed, "Mamā is going to ask her to nurse Lupe until she can take the milk of a cow."

"Tell her to tell the woman that we intend paying her for helping us," said Adam.

"She has already thought of that. Mamā will make it work. We are close to the woman."

Finally, after some hours of mental and emotional fog, reality started to sink in.

"There is a lot to do, Maria," he said, "and little time to do it in."

"Let's go to see *Señor* Pedro. Maybe he can help us find a casket."

"I am sure he can help," she said.

Adam looked at his watch. It was a little past noon.

Pedro was proving himself to be invaluable. Not only was he able to locate a simple, but well-built, wooden casket, but also arranged for two men to deliver it and accompany Adam to *'La Colina de la Muerte,'* the "Hill of the Dead," and dig the grave.

"Maria, Father Lopez needs to be contacted. Can you go while I help Pedro's men?"

"Of course, Adam."

"Ask if he can be here by noon tomorrow."

As Maria was about to mount the little Vespa, two men with the casket and shovels showed up in an old chevy pickup.

"*Hola amigos,*" he said, "*Habla inglés.*"

"*Un poco,*" said one of them.

"Go ahead, Maria, I'll handle things here."

He watched her motor up the street dodging potholes along the way.

"*Ven,*" he said pointing to the casket and motioning the men to bring it inside.

Once inside he moved the chairs around and pointed down: "*Aquí,*" he said.

He glanced over at Floeceta. To him she looked like an angel just asleep. The moment brought him overwhelming despair, but he straightened and motioned the men to follow him to the hill. Once there he looked around trying to find an appropriate spot. His eyes immediately fixed on a place under the big cypress tree. He marked it by striking his heel on the ground.

"*Aquí,*" he said.

After about an hour of digging, each taking turns with the shovel, it was done. Adam couldn't shake the thought; this would be the place where his beloved would remain forever. Her journey in life brought her back to the place it began.

He settled up with the men, Alonzo and Hernan, who seemed to be decent folk. He made arrangements with them to come the next day at noon to help carry the coffin up the hill, lower it in the ground and cover the grave. "Bring rope," he said, miming as if pulling a rope. Alonzo, the English speaker gave a thumbs-up indicating he understood.

Maria met Adam as he was coming off the hill.

"Father Lopez will be here tomorrow at noon," she said.

Together they went to the *casa*. Margarita was there, busying herself by mopping the floor. There was food on the table. On Adam's cot lay Lupe in a cardboard box padded inside with pieces of cloth.

Margarita immediately began talking to Maria, and as usual she translated:

"Dr. Gonzales came today. He was terribly upset and expressed that he wished he could have done more. Also, Moses, your taxi driver friend, gave regret and said for you to call him when you can."

As if ignoring what was relayed to him, he asked:

"Where did Lupe's box come from?"

"I stopped by the grocery store on my way back. My boss gave it to me."

"Where did the food come from?"

"Some neighbors brought it."

He looked at his watch: almost five. Soon, the sun would be setting.

"Let's go back to the hill," he said to Maria.

They trekked the slope, to the place where Florecita would be laid to rest the next day. Once there he picked up a flat rock he had been eyeing. It was about twelve inches by eighteen inches and three inches thick: "This will make a good headstone," he said.

"*Sí*, a good headstone," she repeated, tearing up once more.

Maria was only seventeen, but much older than her years. Adam knew that she had to be in order to survive the environment to which she was destined. Now, she was to be like a little sister that he would need to be protective of.

He held her hand as they watched the sunset, then headed back down to the dim shadowed *casa*.

Adam spent the evening scratching deeply on Florecita's head stone with a rusty nail he had found on the road. It simply read:

Florecita Clay
1991 – 2012

As far as Adam was concerned, there was nothing more to say.

Margarita was exhausted, and retired to her bed shortly after darkness fell. She had to be up early and take Lupe to the relative who had agreed to nurse her. She had managed to scurry up a couple of bottles with nipples and some powdered milk from neighbors. She knew that this milk would not be good for the baby, but it would have to do for the times between nursing. She had also negotiated for some diapers.

Lupe was sleeping in her cardboard crib on a chair next to Maria.

All was quiet. He lay there on his cot next to Florecita's bed. Usually, during this time they would talk and plan with hope for the future. Now, for him, it was a matter of waiting it out…for the dawn…for the moment he would lose every physical trace of her forever.

If only I had insisted on taking her to the hospital when I first got here, preyed on his mind. *If only I could turn back time.*

He lay there, not even expecting sleep. He whiled away the time wondering where she might be. Was she in some far off Heaven, or perhaps she was there…watching…listening, but not being able to make contact. Was there a way to bridge the gap between the worlds of the living and the dead?…he wondered. For the first time in his life he was giving thought to such things.

His deep drifting thoughts were suddenly interrupted. There was movement from Florecita's direction. He watched frozen as she rose from her bed, turned on her side facing him and propped herself on her elbow as he had seen her do many times before:

"Do not be in pain because of me, *mi Amore,*" she said. "I am fine. Now, remember this…I will always be with you, sometimes in your mind… sometimes in your dreams…always in your heart. Take care of our miracle, and my mother and Maria… and Maria." She then began to fade.

He woke in a cold sweat…looked over at her. She lay there…still in the shadows. He looked around the room…nothing unusual. He looked at his watch…11:35. He laid back down and soon drifted into a peaceful dreamless sleep.

He was awakened by Margarita passing through with Lupe, taking her to nurse. It was almost 6:00. Soon afterward Maria came in holding up a lovely white dress.

"Do you think she will look pretty in this," she asked.

"She will be beautiful, Maria."

"Bueno, for it is the only one like this I have."

"No, Maria I want her buried in her gown. Your sister is in another world, now. You are here in this world…of the living. I'm sure she would want you to wear this dress today instead of her."

"It will be as you wish, Adam."

There was a time while waiting for the men to come and take his Florecita to her final resting place that he was alone with her. He walked over to the casket. She lay there, as beautiful as ever. He kissed her lips, then took her hand and gently removed the ring. He placed it on the counter top next to Margarita's hotplate.

It didn't matter that the ceremony was in Spanish. Had it been in English he still would not have heard a word of it. His mind was far in some far off place.

As she was lowered into the ground all of the few there were in tears, including Father Lopez who had conducted the service and delivered the eulogy. Maria wept in a muffled sniffling whimper, Margarita cried aloud. Even Alonzo and Hernan, the grave diggers had their handkerchiefs out... so did Pedro and his wife. He could also hear sobbing from the small group of neighbors standing in the background.

Adam, holding Lupe, stood silent. To him it was like watching a movie...not real...like being lost in a world of suspended disbelief. He held the babe close, convinced that, through her he was feeling the tingle of Flor's life force. He looked down at her. With a wisp of dark hair and per-fect little features, she looked like an ivory doll in the sunlight. She had her mother's eyes: He looked into them: "Are you there?" he whispered. The babe continued looking at him, cooed, and then appeared to smile.

As the last shovel of dirt was thrown on the grave, any hope of solace in the foreseeable future was gone. He no longer felt the tingle.

As those who were there dispersed, he handed the baby to Maria.

"I'll be along shortly," he said.

He paid the grave diggers, and waited until all were gone, then took out his cell phone:

"Connect," he said, "connect."

It did.

"José, this is Adam."

"Hola, Mi Amigo. How are you?"

"Not well…Florecita is gone. She passed away after giving birth to our daughter."

There was dead silence at the other end of the line.

"The strain of the journey here was too much for her."

"No!" cried José.

"They killed her, José."

The signal began to fade.

"Dancy…" was his last word before the connection was lost.

There were no tears left for Adam Clay. It seemed that anger was all that remained at the end of this day.

Chapter 25

Great sadness loomed over the little shanty in the days that followed. Margarita, for the most part, was taking care of Lupe. Maria was back working at the market.

"You don't have to work," he said, "I can take care of us all."

"You are kind, Adam, but I need to stay busy."

He had no interest in returning to the states. This was his family, from this time forward. He planned to stay here, raise his daughter and take care of them.

Now, immersed in a Spanish-speaking world, he began to pick it up fairly quickly. Soon, he and Margarita were carrying on piecemeal conversations.

There was little concern about properly conjugating verbs and so forth. All he wanted was to get his message across. Margarita delighted in correcting him. Sometimes he deliberately mispronounced words just to hear her laugh. "de nader", he would say, instead of "de nada," meaning, "you're welcome." He claimed that he was speaking a southern dialect of Spanish…the way they spoke it in Alabama. She was attempting a little Spanglish herself: "Going to change shits today." Adam didn't correct her, thinking it much more charming to express in that way instead of: 'I'm going to change the sheets today." He called their style of communication, "Me Tarzan, You Jane" talk. All of this afforded a little light-hearted relief from the great loss in their lives. Sometimes, though, in the middle of laughter Margarita would suddenly break down and began to sob. This caused Adam to do the same. It seemed that the sting of loss would not go away. However, Adam would never look upon Margarita the same since witnessing her take control at Lupe's birth. In his eyes, no longer was she the docile little old woman he thought he knew. He now referred to her as '*Margarita de Acero*' (Steel Daisy).

It was past time to contact Justin.

As he walked up the hill and approached Florecita's grave, he felt a great rush of anxiety. His heart raced. He could feel it throbbing in his chest and head. His legs weakened and were giving way. Feeling that he could no longer stand, he sat, then lay down next to her and began to weep.

He cried out: "Why did you have to go? I'm lost without you…but you know that."

As he lay there lost in grief, a gentle breeze came and bathed him. Then, suddenly, the memory of a dream the night after her death came to him.

"Do not be in pain because of me, *mi Amore*," she said. "I am fine. Now, remember this…I will always be with you, sometimes in your mind… sometimes in your dreams…always in your heart. Take care of our miracle, and my mother and Maria…and Maria." He wondered why Maria's name was repeated.

As the breeze began to fade, he felt his strength coming back. He got to his feet, took out his cell phone, and punched in Justin's number.

"Connect, you Son-of-a…."

"Good morning. This is the office of Justin Walker. How may I help you?" said the pleasant voice.

"This is Adam Clay calling from Mexico" he said to the secretary, "May I speak to Mr. Walker, please?"

A few moments passed: "Adam, I'm glad to hear from you. I was starting to worry."

"A lot has happened, Justin."

"Bring me up to date."

"Florecita's dead."

"My God, Adam, what happened?"

"She died during child birth."

"I'm so sorry, my friend."

"What about the baby?"

"She's OK…normal and healthy."

"Are you making it?"

"Yes, but It's been rough, Justin."

"Are you going to reconsider coming back to the states?"

"No, You know I've burned that bridge. I plan to make my life here with Florecita's mother and sister…and the baby, of course."

"What did you name the baby?"

"Florecita named her 'Lupe' just before she died."

"That's a pretty name…I'm so sorry for your loss."

"Well, I can thank Dancy and his bunch. The trip here, after being deported, was too much. It weakened her so that she was never able to recover."

"I can't even imagine how you must feel, but nothing can be done about it now."

"Yeah," Adam replied. "OK, bring me up to speed on what's happening."

"Well, the vehicles are sold, most of the equipment is sold, and the house is on the market."

"Good. I'll be going into the city tomorrow…to Banamax, one of the largest banks down here. I'm going to open an account. I'll call from there when it's done. I'll want you to wire fifty thousand dollars into it. If things work out, we'll start transferring everything."

After hanging up with Justin, he punched in the numbers for Moses.

He looked at his phone: "Connect, baby…"

"Moses, this is Adam."

"Adam, I am saddened by your loss. What can I do for you, *Amigo*?"

"Thank you for your kind thought, Moses. Can you come pick me up tomorrow morning? I need to go into town?"

"*Sí*…at what time?"

"As soon as you can."

"The soonest will probably be around nine."

"That's good. I'll be ready."

He put the phone in his pocket, looked over at Florecita's grave, blew a kiss, and started down the slope.

Upon arrival to the *casa*: "Maria, I need you to go into town with me tomorrow. We have some business to take care of."

"As you wish, Adam…but for what reason?"

"I'm going to set up an account with Banamax. I want you on it with me."

"I have never had a bank account. I do not even know to write a check."
Adam smiled: "Don't worry; you'll learn."

Moses showed up a little after nine the next morning. As he navigated through the downtown traffic, Adam took notice of a small band of young boys roaming the streets. He knew from Father Lopez that these were "the street children of Mexico City" …the unwanted…the outcast of this society.

His mind took a temporary detour from the mission at hand: But for the grace of God, he thought, Leonardo Lopez would still be wandering the avenues, washing windshields at traffic lights for a couple of pesos, and sleeping in the sewers. Fate has its way, he contemplated.

Finally, after fighting downtown traffic for almost an hour, they pulled up in front of Banamax, a large modern building in the heart of the city.

"Call me when you have finished," said Moses, "and I will come as soon as possible."

Inside its lobby, Banamax looked very much like a typical American bank, with a little touch of Mexico here and there. Adam and Maria walked to one of the teller windows.

"I need to set up a checking account," said Adam in English.

"One moment," said the young lady, also in English.

She picked up her phone: "Mr. Cortez, A gentleman is here to open an account."

Within moments an immaculately dressed man of dark complexion and somewhere in his forty's appeared.

"He held out his hand: "I am Ricardo Cortez, Señor. How can I help you?"

I'm Adam Clay. This is Maria Valdez, my sister-in-law. We need to set up a checking account."

"Good: come with me, please," he said, ushering them into his private office.

"How much would you like put into your new account?"

"One thousand dollars, initially; however I need to contact my attorney in the states to wire an additional fifty thousand dollars when the account is set up: May I use your phone once we're done?"

"Of course, Mr. Clay."

A mailing address was asked for during the application process.

Ricardo's eyebrows rose when Adam handed him a piece of paper with the address written on it.

"Don't send anything to this address, though," said Adam, "for obvious reasons."

"Yes, I understand…and agree," said Ricardo.

"I'll set up a post office box today," said Adam, "and call you with a P.O. number where monthly statements and any correspondence can be sent."

"We'll come back and pick up the check books when they are printed and ready."

"*Sí, Señor*, I will have everything done as soon as possible."

With the paperwork finished, Adam placed his call to Justin:

"Justin, Adam here."

"Hi, Adam. What's happening…or should I say, *Que pasa?*"

"The account is set up," said Adam, "and we're ready for you to wire the fifty thousand. I'm going to put Mr. Ricardo Cortez on the line. He'll instruct you on how to do it."

On the way back to Lola Land, after taking care of business in the city, Adam mentioned to Moses: "We need a vehicle. Do you know anyone who is honest enough for me to deal with?"

"As a matter of fact I do. My cousin, Joaquín (*Wa-keen*) is in the business. He will treat you right."

Adam let out a little chuckle: "I believe you have a cousin for everything, Moses."

"Sí, I do. Some are real and some are not."

"Maybe one day I'll become one of your cousins."

"Perhaps," said Moses. They both laughed.

"Joaquín is real, though," said Moses, "He is partly how I know about Alabama. He goes there, buys vehicles and brings them back here to sell."

"If you will, mention to him that I would like to find a low mileage Jeep Cherokee. That's what I'm used to driving."

"That I will do, Amigo."

Maria quietly peered out the window during the conversation, her thoughts obviously elsewhere.

"What are you thinking about, Maria?" asked Adam.

"Oh, just about everything that has happened."

"Well, what do you think about us getting an automobile?"

"I do not know how to drive."

"You'll learn."

"It appears I have many things to learn."

He looked over at her and smiled, then put his hand on top of hers and gave a brief, gentle squeeze. She looked back and returned the smile.

Chapter 26

In days that followed, Adam spent a lot of time on the hill where his Florecita was laid to rest. On this day, as usual, he lay down next to her grave. On his back, he peered into the cobalt blue sky scattered with large-snow white cumulus clouds. He could have sworn he saw her face in the one directly above. Then, the same gentle breeze as before came. It lingered for a while, then slowly died down. To him, the breeze was their way of speaking with one another…in silent words.

"I have to get the family out of this place, my love. I don't want to leave you, but I know this is what you want, too.

"Lupe is fine. Your mother is spoiling her, though. Maria is still trying to cope with losing you…just as I am. Sometimes when she smiles she reminds me of you."

He began to well up as he always did when this close to her grave. "I miss you terribly, my Love."

The breeze rose again: then slowly died down.

He wiped away the tears: "I better go now," he said, "I need to get some diapers for our little miracle. Her plumbing works very good.

"Rest well, *mí Amor…. Mí Corazón.*"

As he began his trek down the hill, the breeze rose again briefly, then all went to a peaceful calm.

Margarita was anxious to try out the disposal diapers that had been special ordered. Maria would be working until 5:00; so Adam volunteered to go pick them up earlier during the day.

It was early afternoon before he began his walk towards the little market. Hopefully, the diapers would be there and ready for him to pick up.

Along the way there was an isolated stretch where no buildings resided…only a few gnarled trees and scrub brush. Four young men approached from the opposite direction. They looked to be somewhere in their twenties. As they got closer, Adam's instincts kicked in. Just by their body language he knew there was a good possibility that there was going to be an incident.

"*Buenas tardes, Señor*," said the pocked face hombre who was obviously the leader.

"*Hola*," said Adam, hoping that would be it, and everyone would be on their way…but no such luck.

He held out his hand: "*da me un cigarillo, Señor Gringo*."

Though all of them were lean and undoubtedly tough, none were big. He knew the only way to deal with a situation such as this was through a show of strength and authority.

He swelled himself, and glared at the leader: "*No tengo*," he said in the most authoritative voice he could muster.

"*Entonces su dinero, Señor*."

The brash aggressor kept closing in on him.

"Back off," Adam growled. But, he kept coming.

Without further warning, Adam lashed out. His fist landed on the agitator's jaw sending him sailing backwards and to the ground. The others swarmed in and started hitting and kicking. He fought back with an adrenalin-fueled anger. Everything held inside now surfaced…everything.

Even though he was throwing blows that sent some of the young thugs reeling like bowling pins, he was receiving a beating. There was no feeling of pain until a sharp one came from an area around his shoulder, and then his side, and then his back.

He was weakening. The swarm was too much. He felt himself going to the ground. Then came the kick to his head. Beyond that, he had no recollection…until:

He heard a voice in the distance: "Adam…Adam." Someone was definitely calling him, but he couldn't tell from where. He opened his eyes. Slowly, she came into focus. His head was cradled in Maria's arms: "Adam, please be alright," she kept repeating. He had been lying there in the dust and the dirt on the side of the road, unconscious for how long, he didn't know.

He raised his arm and reached up. Two fingers touched her lips: "I'll be alright," he said, not knowing if that was so or not.

His body was stiff and he was feeling a great deal of pain. He knew he had been stabbed, but didn't see that much blood. 'Must not be too bad, he thought. Then it hit him. In near panic he grabbed at his waist. Thank God, he thought. They didn't get my belt.

"We must get you home," she said, "We must go now…the sun is setting fast."

With her help he struggled to his feet. There on the ground lay his wallet. She picked it up and handed it to him. The two hundred fifty pesos were gone, but everything else was there. It occurred to him that for less than twenty bucks they were willing to kill.

They mounted the Vespa. With Adam holding on the best he could, they were off. His body took another beating from every bump and pothole along the way. All he could do was grit his teeth and cling to Maria.

Even though it was only minutes, to Adam it seemed like a much longer ride before arriving home. Margarita helped get him inside and to Florecita's bed. He lay there motionless as they began peeling his clothes off. Now, swollen with blackened eyes and burises clearly visible on his face…he moaned as they turned him over to remove the bloody shirt. Burning pains mounted in his shoulder, back and side. Every movement was excruciating. The pounding ache in his head was almost a relief that took away from some of the other discomforts. As they examined the stab wounds; Margarita, in Spanish, said, "We must get a '*curandero*' (curer – community healer) to look at these wounds." They turned him back over.

"Remove his shoes and socks," said Margarita as she unbuckled his belt, then unbuttoned and unzipped his jeans. She slipped her hands under his back and levered him up: "Pull them off." She ordered.

As he groaned, Maria tugged until the jeans slipped off. Margarita carefully inspected his legs looking for injuries. Then, in an unexpected motion she pulled off his jockey shorts and started examining as if at the market looking for unwanted bruises on a tomato. For all practical purposes immobilized, he could not have resisted even if he wanted to. Adding to it all, he couldn't help but take notice of Maria looking on with unusual curiosity.

Perhaps, he thought, she had never seen the private parts of an adult male before. At this point it really didn't matter. This was no time to worry about modesty. He lay there on his back naked until Margarita placed a towel across him. She then headed out the door to fetch the community healer.

"Can I get you anything, Adam," asked Maria.

"I have to go to the bathroom."

As she was helping him up the baby started crying.

"She needs changing," said Maria.

"Like father, like daughter," he said.

She looked at him in a puzzled way.

It would have hurt too much for him to laugh:

"Go," he said

The towel hit the floor. Maria went to change the baby, and Adam, cursing under his breath, hobbled to the bathroom.

After at least a half-hour of agony as the stab wounds were cleaned with alcohol and dressed, Jesus, the community 'curer', proclaimed that the patient would survive. The back wound, he said, was not deep enough to puncture the lung; the side cut was deep but grazed the gut and missed the vitals. And, the shoulder was no more than a nasty puncture.

"*Beba esta para el dolor*" (drink this for pain) he said, putting a cup filled with some concoction to Adam's lips.

Shortly after the wound-cleansing ordeal and taking a few sips of the bitter pain medicine prepared and prescribed by the curer, Adam fell into deep sleep, unaware of anything except for the few times during the night that he felt a wet rag touch his face and forehead.

He awoke when the shaft of morning light beamed through the room's only window and illuminated the wall where Christ hung on the cross, and Mother Mary, hands clasped, looked angelically towards the ceiling. He was so stiff and sore he could barely move his arm, much less reposition himself. His eyes were almost swollen shut. He lay there and waited…for what he didn't know. It was the first time he could remember being unable to do for himself…an unpleasant situation for a man as independent and self-sufficient as Adam Clay to be in.

Soon, Maria came into the room: "How are you, Adam?"

"Not too good…can you bring me a mirror?"

"Are you sure?"

"Yes, I want to see."

As suspected his face was a mess…eyes and cheeks swollen, black and blue with a large lump on his forehead. At least, he thought, he still had his teeth, and his nose wasn't broken.

"Are you hungry?" she asked.

"No, I can't seem to muster up an appetite for some reason," he said sarcastically.

She stared at him with a puzzled look as she had several times before. Even in this sorry state he found this little trait of hers appealing.

The day after the incident was rough…much pain and misery, but the day after that was even worse. By the third day things seemed to be getting a little better.

During this time he lay there with nothing but a sheet covering him. It made it easier for Margarita to monitor and dress his wounds. Only with the help of a wooden staff provided by, Jesus, the curer, was he able to make it to the bathroom. A shower was out of the question.

That evening Margarita instructed Maria to give him a sponge bath while she mended clothes and darned socks in the other room. Maria came with a sponge and bowl of warm water. The room was dimly lit… not much light could be expected from a ceiling fixture with a sixty watt bulb screwed into it.

Modesty had become a casualty of necessity; so Adam decided to close his eyes and relax. The warm water felt good as she gently patted around his cheeks, eyes and forehead. She squeezed the sponge and let water drip on his three-day-old beard before drying with a cloth.

He felt the sheet being pulled down to a little below his waist. The wet sponge came close but never touched the shoulder wound. It moved lightly over his chest and then his stomach. He could hear her squeezing it into the bowl, then letting it soak up more water.

He felt the sponge lying on his stomach and her hand somewhere below his navel. Then suddenly, unexpectedly, he felt her lips press to his. He didn't twitch or move an inch...nor did he open his eyes. Only a moment had passed before Margarita called out from the other room:

"Maria, come, *por favor*. I need you to try on this dress."

She didn't come back that evening, and nothing was mentioned by either of them the next day...or any day thereafter.

Chapter 27

After a week of being mostly bed-ridden, Adam began to feel as if he could function. He needed to start taking care of business again. Though still sore, swollen and with pain from his wounds, he managed to make it up the hill.

After spending a few silent moments standing above his beloved Florecita's head stone, he punched in Moses's number. It connected.

"Moses, this is Adam."

"Adam, *mí Amigo*, I have good news. Joaquin (*Wa-keen)* arrived a few days ago with a Jeep Cherokee."

"Good," said Adam, "When can I see it?"

"I will give you his number."

Realizing that his memory was still a little off, Adam scratched the number in the dirt with a stick. Immediately after hanging up with Moses he punched it in. Luck was with him again.

"*Bueno*," said the voice at the other end.

"Joaquin, this is Adam Clay, Moses's friend. He said you have a Jeep Cherokee I might be interested in."

"*Sí, Señor*, I just brought it in from the states a few days ago. It has forty-five thousand miles and is in excellent condition. Someone took very good care of this vehicle."

"When can I see it?' asked Adam.

"Now, if you like."

"Where do I need to come?"

"I will bring it to you."

"I'm sorry, but I don't know how to tell you to get here.

"Don't worry, Moses will give me directions."

Adam, excited, almost forgot his pain as he made his way down the hill.

Within the hour it rolled to a stop in front of the *casa*. He looked hard at the vehicle and did a double take. A chill went up his spine. The color… dark olive, tinted windows, sunroof. *This can't be*, shot through his mind. He looked again…in detail…walked around it. There it was, the large ding on the passenger's side door delivered by some careless ass-hole in a parking lot.

"Where did it come from?" asked Adam.

"Alabama," answered Joaquin as he handed over the keys, "Start her up, *Señor*. She runs like a fine watch."

Adam opened the door and sat in the all too-familiar seat. He turned on the ignition and checked the mileage…forty-five thousand three hundred and twenty. That would be about right if driven from Alabama. It was somewhere around forty-two thousand when he was last in it.

He started it up. As Joaquin said, it ran like a fine watch…still. Adam had taken particularly good care of the vehicle as he did with all things he owned.

"How much?" he asked.

"Fifteen-thousand American dollars, *Señor*."

Adam knew that Justin sold it at auction for nine thousand dollars.

"I'll give you Twelve thousand…today…in cash."

Adam tried to keep a poker face, but still bruised and swollen it was difficult to project anything but a pathetic suffering Gringo. And, in the meantime Margarita came outside with Lupe which disrupted the rhythm of the deal making.

"I cannot take that little, *Señor*."

"Well, let's split it…thirteen thousand five-hundred."

"Fourteen thousand," said Joaquin.

Adam knew that was high, but he wanted his jeep back…regardless.

"OK, we've got a deal. Let's go to Banamax, my bank, and get it done.

Along the way, Adam asked: "Is Moses really your cousin."

Sí, his mother's brother married my father's sister. Well, actually she was my father's stepsister because…*Sí*, Moses is my cousin.

As they drove through the traffic, the pollution and chaos of Mexico City, Adam remarked:

"I'm going to move my family out of this place. Do you have any ideas where I should be looking?"

"I live in Cuernavaca, a town about eighty kilometers south of here. It is relatively peaceful, the air is good and traffic tolerable. It is never too hot or too cold…and by the way, it has a Walmart."

"I think there's probably a freakin' Walmart on the moon," said Adam."

Joaquin looked over at Adam and smiled. "Probably so," he said.

They drove a little farther without conversation, until Joaquin asked:

"What happened to you, *Señor*…your face?"

"I was attacked and robbed by a gang. That's one reason I want to get me and my family the hell out of here."

"If you are interested, I can show you the area where I live. I think you would like it."

"Yes, I am interested. When can we go?"

"I was planning to take a bus back to Cuernavaca if you bought the jeep. You can drive me home after we complete the transaction if you have time."

"I've got nothing but time. Let's do it," said Adam.

After finally finding a parking place, they entered the Banamax lobby.

"I am Adam Clay here to see *Señor* Cortez. Is he available?"

In a few moments Ricardo Cortez appeared:

"Ahh, Mr. Clay, It is good to see you. My, it appears you've had an accident."

"Yes, but I'm getting better, thank you. This is Mister Joaquin…I'm sorry I don't even know your last name."

"Sanchez," he said, "Joaquin Sanchez."

"I am purchasing a vehicle from Joaquin, and need to withdraw Fourteen thousand U.S. dollars."

"*Sí*, I will have a cashiers check prepared."

"I prefer cash, *Señor*," said Joaquin Joaquin

"Ricardo raised his eye brow: "As you wish, *Señor*."

After the money changed hands, Joaquin pulled a bill-of-sale from his brief case.

"I will go with you to have this properly recorded," he said while filling it out.

"I have your checkbooks ready, Mr. Clay…and by the way, Mr. Walker called last week trying to reach you. He said that it was very important that you see an email he sent. You are welcome to use one of our computers if you like."

"Thank you," said Adam, but I'll have to check it later. We have a lot to do before the day is over."

Finally, they were on their way to Cuernavaca. It was a pleasant drive, and scenic, too.

The highway was good, and not too crowded. It was rural along the way, but the shanty's that dotted the hillsides seemed more pastoral than poverty ridden as in the city. As they got closer to their destination, the rolling hills and pastures slowly gave way to higher ground…then even higher until reaching a peak that overlooked a spectacular valley where the small city spread itself out.

"Cuernavaca is called The City of Eternal Spring," said Joaquin.

They descended into the valley, and Adam was given a tour of the area. The town was a mixture of old and new. Joaquin took him to a very old and large family friendly park, then to a modern Holiday Inn. He got a good feeling about this place:

"Do you think a Gringo could get a job here," he asked.

"I definitely think so," said Joaquin, "Are you ready to go to my place?"

"Sure," said Adam.

He drove a short distance to a quiet alley more or less on the outskirts of town. Joaquin drove up to the gate of a solid eight-foot wooden fence. It looked like a stockade from the outside.

He opened the gate. Inside the compound were three two-story brick buildings, each about thirty by sixty feet. They were not new, nor luxury, but very sturdy looking. There was a concrete in-ground swimming pool in front.

"Are these condos?" asked Adam.

"*Sí*, condominiums."

Joaquin opened the door to his ground floor unit. "*Ya llegué*," he called out. Immediately, a little dark haired girl, about four years old, came running from the back.

"*Pa, Pa*," she shouted.

With her arms stretched out, he picked her up, kissed her and held her to him.

"This is my friend, *Señor* Adam," he said.

She looked at Adam, shyly smiled, then buried her head in her father's chest.

He couldn't help but think, is this what I can look forward to? He felt himself swell with emotion.

Then, from the back came a slightly plump but attractive woman, probably in her early thirties.

"Rosa, this is *Señor* Adam Clay. I am going to show him around."

"Welcome to our home, *Señor*."

Adam nodded, "*Gracious, Señoria*."

As they walked through the house, Adam took notice of its construction: "This place is built to last," he said

"Construction in Mexico is different than in the states," said Joaquin, "A brick house here is built totally of brick. In the states what is considered a brick house is framed in wood with only a brick veneer."

The place was not fancy, but well laid out and functional, even in the critical mind of Adam Clay, the architect. It featured a nice size living room, a dining room, an adequately equipped galley kitchen, three bedrooms, two baths plus a washroom and patio.

"I like your place very much," said Adam, "Something like this would be perfect for my family."

"Come with me, *Amigo*," said Joaquin.

They walked outside and over about fifty feet to the next building. Joaquin took a ring of keys from his pocket, picked one and opened the door.

He waved his hand towards the open entry: "After you," he said.

It was obviously unoccupied, but fully furnished. The floor plan was identical to that of Joaquin's place.

"I can rent this to you, fully furnished, for five thousand pesos a months. That's less than four hundred U.S. dollars."

"You own this?" asked Adam.

"*Sí*, I own this building, and the one I live in."

"Yes," said Adam without a blink or hesitation, "I will take it. When can I move my family in?"

"Anytime you wish."

After signing the lease and writing a check for the first month's rent, Joaquin handed Adam two keys…one to the unit and one to the gate.

As he was fixing to head back north to Mexico City he couldn't resist:

"Joaquin, I used to own this vehicle."

"I know," came the reply. "I saw your name in the chain of title when I purchased it. I also know you were an architect and homebuilder in the states. One of Moses's many talents is getting information out of people. By the way, he thinks highly of you.

"He and I are in the process of purchasing land here in Cuernavaca to build houses on. We will discuss this more when you get settled in here."

All sorts of ideas and possibilities bounced around in Adam's head as he headed north on Hwy. 95D: Maybe there is opportunity for me in Cuernavaca, he thought. Joaquin had even hinted at it. He was an entrepreneur who seemed to know construction and was already involved in real estate. Maybe…just maybe there was opportunity waiting in the 'City of Eternal Spring'. Hell, he thought, we just may all end up being cousins… me, Moses and Joaquin.

It was almost dark when Adam rolled up in the new purchase. Maria ran out, obviously excited and asked, "Is it ours?"

"*Sí*, it's ours."

She jumped up and down, wringing her hands like a giddy teenager. He was a little surprised to see the otherwise reserved Maria let go. But, he was finding out that she was full of surprises. And, of course, she was a teenager.

Margarita came out holding Lupe. The first thing she did was open the back door and sit down there. She laid the baby down in the seat next to her. Seemingly satisfied that transporting her precious cargo would work; she looked up through the window at Adam, smiled and gave a thumbs up.

It had been a long day and the lingering pains of Adam's injuries were beginning to take their toll. He laid down in Florecita's bed , which had become sacred to all, and quickly drifted into a deep sleep, dreaming, of course, of her.

Chapter 28

He woke early, before the shaft of daylight beamed through the window. While the others were still fast asleep, he eased out of bed. What caused him to wake was the flash of a memory. Ricardo Cortez said that Justin Walker had sent an important email to him.

Stiff and sore, he stretched until feeling limber enough to dress and set out on the day's missions, first of which was to find an area that had wi-fi in order to retrieve Justin's email. He went into the other room and woke Maria just enough to tell her he was leaving, then grabbed his laptop on the way out.

Dawn was just breaking when he started the jeep and headed out. His destination was a Walmart located at *Plaza Ciudad Jardin,* the one José used to send money monthly to the family for rent and food. The arrangement was that Pedro would pick up the funds, deduct the rent owed him and disperse the rest to the family.

Traffic was light. He arrived there in less than half an hour. Luck was with him. The first attempt to log in was successful. He was on the Internet, then his mailbox. There were over two hundred unread e-mails. He scanned until going back almost two weeks finally finding the one sent by Justin. He opened it. It read:

Adam,
The attachment herein is a scanned copy
of the front page of yesterday's
Montgomery Advertiser.
Regards,
Justin

Adam opened the attachment. He starred at the headline for a moment, it not quite registering. Then, he felt a jolt go through him like a lightning bolt.

J.R. DANCY MURDERED

J. Roland Dancy, prominent Montgomery attorney and political insider, was found murdered in an alley close to his downtown office. His throat was cut in a brutal fashion. No money was taken which ruled out robbery as a motive. It appears to have been a revenge killing say authorities. They say they have no suspects at this time. No known witnesses nor forensic evidence was found at the crime scene...

He closed and saved the email, then immediately punched in José's number:

"*Bueno,*"

"José, Adam here."

"*Hola, mí Amigo. Que pasa?*"

"I just found out about Dancy."

"*Sí,* I understand he was sent to meet his maker."

"Yes, and that's all I want to know about it."

"*Sí,* me too."

"Good."

"How are my mother and sister...and my new niece?"

"They're fine. I've found a good place to live and raise Lupe, in Cuernavaca. I plan to move the family there. Are you OK with that?"

"I trust your judgment, of course, Adam."

"Don't send any more money down here. I've got things covered for now. I'll call if I need anything...OK?"

"OK, but keep in touch."

"I will...how are You, Juan and the boys doing?"

"We're alright for now...staying under the radar...building decks, doing repairs and additions."

"Good enough. I'll call when we get settled in. Take care now."

"*Adios,* Adam."

Immediately, after disconnecting with José, Adam punched in Justin's home number. It was too early for him to be in the office:

"Hello"

"Justin, This is Adam."

"Adam, I've been trying to get in touch with you. What's going on?"

"Sorry Justin, but I've been laid up. I got the crap beat out of me by some thugs a week ago. I've sort of lost track of time."

"Are you OK?"

"Slowly but surely getting better. The bastards stabbed me, too. It's going to take a little longer to get back to normal."

"Damn, I hope you get better soon. Have you read the email I sent you, yet?"

"Yeah, I just read it. Looks like somebody took care of some unfinished business, but I don't need or want to know anything beyond that.

"Neither, I. We'll just let it be."

"I'm moving the family to Cuernavaca," said Adam, "a town about fifty miles south of Mexico City. It seems to be a good place to settle, and there may be some job opportunities for me there."

"OK, my friend, let me know when you get situated."

"Will do. Take care, Justin."

It was still early…approaching eight o'clock, but traffic was increasing by the minute. Adam had noticed a car lot on his way there that also had some small to medium-size utility trailers for sale. He pulled in.

A beer-bellied mustached *hombre* wearing a straw panama hat, carrying a cup of coffee came out of his sales hut.

"What can I do for you, *Señor*?"

"How much are you asking for your utility trailer?" asked Adam pointing to one that was about the size of a pickup truck bed.

"I can sell it to you for five thousand pesos, *Señor*."

"I will give you four thousand pesos cash, hook it up to my vehicle and take it off the lot right now."

"No can do, *Señor*…maybe four thousand five hundred."

"Ok," said Adam, thank you for your time, anyway."

He got back into the jeep, closed the door and started the engine.

"Wait," said the *hombre*, "I'll take your offer, *Señor*."

It was almost ten before Adam made it home, the trailer in tow. He went inside where Margarita was cleaning and Maria attending Lupe.

"We are leaving this place tomorrow," he said, "I have found very good place for us in Cuernavaca."

Both women looked at him with a surprised gaze.

"*Oué*," said Maria.

"We're moving to Cuernavaca. It will be a new start for us as a family. It's where we need to be."

"But this is our home," said Maria.

"This place is bad…bad for all of us. Trust me, you will like it there. You'll even have your own bedroom, Maria."

He looked at Margarita: "Are you OK with this, Mamacita?"

She smiled: "*Tú eres el jefe de esta familia*" (You are the head of this family), she said. "You know what is best. We go where you say go."

Maria then smiled and nodded in agreement: "I only regret having to leave my sister here," she said.

"I feel the same, but I know this is what she would want us to do. It will mean a much better life for all of us."

"*Si*," she replied.

"The place we are going to has everything we need…couches, tables, chairs, beds, pots and pans…everything. We'll take what will fit in the jeep and trailer…and leave the rest. You need to go and tell Pedro that we will not be here after tomorrow. He can have whatever we leave. Also, tell them at the market that you are leaving. That would be the right thing to do."

As each busied herself, Adam began digging up the daisies he had planted in front of what he now called *la casa pequeño* (the little house). He carefully put them in containers and watered them well. After finishing he made his way with them up the hill where Florecita was. With great care he planted them all around her headstone:

"We're leaving tomorrow, *mi Amor*," he said after completing the task, "I may never be able to come back to this place again. I just don't know… but what I do know is I will always love you. And, I promise to do the best I can with our little miracle."

He could have sworn he felt the breeze rise and fall, but wasn't sure if it was real or imagined.

He went to the big cypress tree that shaded her grave, patted its trunk: "Take care big guy," he said, then headed back down the hill.

A lot of the day was spent arguing about what was to go and what was to stay. Adam was having difficulty trying to convince Margarita not to take her hot plate: "Mamacita" he said, "You will have a real stove that will cook three times as much and twice faster."

But, she kept insisting. "It has been with me always," she argued.

Finally, he gave up… and, deep down understood. It went into the 'go' pile along with her pots and pans. All agreed, however, that Florecita's bed was to go. It would become Lupe's bed when she was older.

Margarita wanted also to take her bed. Adam didn't bother to argue. The jeep was filling up fast but there would be enough room in the trailer, even after the Vespa was loaded.

Even though it was the only home she had ever known, Maria had no attachments to anything in Lola Land…no friends, no social interaction nor really any hope of escape. For her, it had only been an exercise in survival. Now, she was just anxious to leave.

The day was drawing to a close and most everything was done.

"Let's go to the hill," he said to both Margarita and Maria.

Holding hands, they stood looking down at her small headstone with freshly planted daisies around it, bidding final farewell to their beloved Florecita, each in their own way…each with their own memories. All was quiet except for Margarita's whispered prayers. Adam, holding the baby, had earlier that day spent his private time there. Even so, emotions of the moment surfaced as he observed the sadness around him. A lump came to his throat as he listened to Maria's whimpers. He was well aware that Florecita, her big sister, had been her protector when she was a little girl…and her ideal when growing up. There were so many shared plans and dreams that had gone unfulfilled.

Adam took notice. There definitely was no breeze this time…none to rise and fall in silent words. It's time to go, he thought...time to rest...for both the quick and the dead.

The shaft of morning light beamed through the room's only window. It reflected on an empty wall. 'Jesus on the cross' and 'Mother Mary' had been removed and carefully wrapped...ready for transport.

It was time to make the journey...begin the new adventure, but first there would be a shave and shower. Sleepy-eyed Maria was just waking up. Margarita was already outside, organizing and re-organizing things in the jeep.

By ten o'clock, everything had been loaded up, buttoned up and all were ready to depart. Margarita, with Lupe was the first to get situated in the jeep. Lupe's cardboard box crib took up half of the back seat.

Standing there, breathing in the last they would in this place, Adam looked into lovely Maria's dark eyes.

"Let's go," he said.

As they traveled the dusty pothole-riddled road out of Lola Land, Adam saw something all too familiar ahead. Walking along the side of the road was the gang of four that attacked him two weeks before.

His first impulse was to ram them, and keep doing so until they became a part of the rubble so fitting of this place. He looked in the rear view mirror and took a brief glance at Margarita holding Lupe in the back seat, then over at Maria.

He pulled up beside the group, stopped, and rolled down the window. He glared at them. They all looked stunned, and postured themselves to run. Upon quick assessment he saw the scabs and left over bruises...remnants of the damage he himself had been able to inflict.

He stared hard at each of them:

"*Buenos días Caballeros,*" he said. Then, after allowing himself a contemptuous smile and flick of the wrist pointing forward, he drove off.

He looked in the rear view mirror as the pathetic squalor, sad inhabitants, and hard memories of Lola Land were being left behind. He put his arm out the window, reached as high as he could and in the moment before making an intended obscene gesture, he instead pointed skyward, spread his fingers and let the air flow through and around his hand. He felt the gravity of Lola Land weaken as they made their way out. Their heading, now, was the future…and hope.

There was much to leave behind in the life of Adam Clay, but never ever would he leave that place in his heart and mind where once a flower grew.

9 780966 136517